My First Picture Dictionary

Scott, Foresman and Company

EDITORIAL OFFICES: Glenview, Illinois

REGIONAL OFFICES: Sunnyvale, California · Tucker, Georgia
Glenview, Illinois · Oakland, New Jersey · Dallas, Texas

ISBN: 0-673-12489-4
ISBN: 0-673-28452-2

12345678910-KPK-989796959493929190

Contents

Introduction

My First Picture Dictionary is an attractive and colorful book of words and pictures for beginning readers and writers. It is designed for those children who have advanced beyond the picture-book level, and introduces them to the idea of using a reference book. *My First Picture Dictionary* prepares children for the transition to an actual dictionary by familiarizing them with simple dictionary skills.

My First Picture Dictionary is written for children who know the alphabet and have had some experience alphabetizing letters and words. Therefore, the words in the book are listed in alphabetical order. Each entry word is listed in large, heavy type. A simple definition is given for each entry word, with the exception of function words, such as *the* and *what,* and irregular inflected forms. The entry word is then used in a sentence. Inflected forms such as noun plurals, verb forms, and adjective forms are given at the end of the entry. In addition, each irregular inflected form is given separate entry.

Approximately 75 percent of the words in *My First Picture Dictionary* are illustrated. Original art, photographs, cartoons, and fine art are used to picture the word being defined. A caption, always the same as the entry word for easy reference, accompanies each illustration. All illustrations are adjacent to the word they picture.

The 1500 entries in *My First Picture Dictionary* were chosen from a list of words that children who are learning to read and write will encounter in school and at home. Numerous books for beginning readers (including reading, language arts, handwriting, science, health, mathematics, and social studies texts) were read and their vocabulary was analyzed to make up the word list. In addition, all Dolch List words,

many of them function words, are listed. Names of things children commonly encounter in their homes and neighborhoods are also included.

At the back of the book is a section called "Find Out the Facts!" Its colorfully illustrated pages contain useful information on shapes, the human body, nutrition, maps, numbers, measurement, telling time, the calendar, holidays, opposites, and colors.

Scott, Foresman and Company has been a leader in producing quality children's dictionaries for over fifty years. *My First Picture Dictionary* was prepared by an experienced team of editors, designers, and illustrators. Throughout its development and production, a panel of primary teachers served as project advisers.

People use dictionaries not only in school, but throughout their entire lifetime. Gaining access to the information contained in dictionaries is therefore an important learning experience. In using *My First Picture Dictionary,* young children take the first steps toward acquiring basic dictionary skills.

A 16-page teacher's guide to using *My First Picture Dictionary* is available on request.

The Editors

How to Read an Entry

Several sample entries are printed below.
Explanations of the parts of an entry
appear in the boxes.

The entry word is in a separate column so it is easy to find. It is printed in heavy black type. It shows you how the word is spelled.

The small raised number tells you that two different entry words with different meanings have the same spelling.

A sentence shows how the word is used.

A sentence tells you the meaning of the word.

A picture helps to show the meaning of the word. Each picture has a caption that is the same as the entry word.

A number is printed before each meaning of a word when more than one meaning is given.

top¹

top¹ Top means the highest part. We saw the **top** of the mountain. **tops.**

top² A top is a toy that spins. The **top** went round and round. **tops.**

top²

trip 1. When you go on a **trip**, you travel from one place to another. Let's take a **trip** to the ocean. **trips.**
2. Trip also means to fall. I tripped on the rope. **tripped, tripping.**

true True means right or correct. It is true that 4 and 6 are 10. A true story is not made up. **truer, truest.**

Word endings and special forms of entry words come at the end of the entry. They are printed in heavy black type.

Aa

a   Pat has **a** red hat. Do you have **a** book on cats? Thanksgiving comes once **a** year.

able   If you are **able** to do something, it means that you can do it. Jan is **able** to walk on her hands.

able

about   I like stories **about** animals. Bob and Sue are **about** the same size. I have **about** finished my homework.

above   The red bird is on the branch **above** the blue bird.

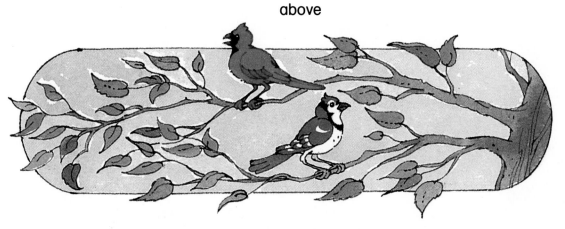

above

across   Maria walked **across** the street to play with her friends.

act   **Act** means to pretend you are someone else. Lee **acted** the part of the wolf in the play. **acted, acting.**

act

add   **Add** means to put things together. When you **add**, you find how much or how many. She **added** 2 and 3 to make 5. **added, adding.**

adult   An **adult** is a grown-up person. Your teacher is an **adult. adults.**

adult

7

A | a

after

after   The dog ran **after** the ball. Four comes **after** five.

afternoon   **Afternoon** is the part of day between morning and evening. We played ball this **afternoon** after school. **afternoons.**

again

again   When you do something once more, you do it **again**. Beth tried **again** and got the right answer.

age   Your **age** is the number of years you have lived. Sam started school at the **age** of five.

ahead

ahead   The girl in red was **ahead** of all the other runners. Go **ahead** with your work.

air   The **air** we breathe is all around us. It has no smell, taste, or color. The **air** above us is called the sky.

airplane

airplane   An **airplane** is a machine that can fly. **Airplanes** have wings and engines. **airplanes.**

airport

airport   An **airport** is a place where airplanes land and take off. **airports.**

alike   When things are **alike**, they are like one another. When things are **alike**, they are not different. The twins look **alike.**

alike

alive   When something is **alive**, it has life and is living. The snake was badly hurt, but it was still **alive.**

 all

all   All the children are smiling. The mice ate **all** the cheese.

alligator   An **alligator** is a large animal with thick skin. It has a very large mouth and a long tail. **Alligators** live in warm rivers. **alligators.**

alligator

9

A | a

almost

almost   I **almost** missed the bus. It is **almost** ten o'clock.

alone   **Alone** means without anyone else. He sat **alone** because he didn't know the other children.

alone

along

along   Trees are planted **along** the street. We took our dog **along**.

alphabet   The **alphabet** is all the letters from A to Z. Can you say the **alphabet**?

alphabet

already   She has **already** read this book. Her father said she had **already** left for school.

also   Sam has a dog, but he likes cats **also**.

always   Always eat a good breakfast before you go to school.

am   Today I **am** seven years old.

amount   The **amount** of something is how much there is or how many there are. The **amount** of milk Jan needs for the soup is one cup. One dollar is a small **amount** of money. **amounts.**

amount

an   There is **an** apple in the basket, and a banana too. I ate **an** egg and two pieces of toast.

and

and   His hat **and** mittens are blue. 4 **and** 2 make 6. Sue **and** Lee played a game.

angry   When you are upset and not pleased about something, you are **angry**. Dad was **angry** when I broke the window. **angrier, angriest.**

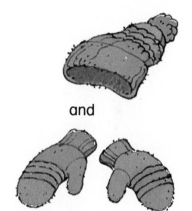

angry

A | a

animal   Any living thing that can move about is an **animal. Animals** cannot make their own food from sunlight as plants do. People, dogs, birds, fish, ants, and worms are **animals. animals.**

animal

ankle

ankle   The **ankle** is the part of the body between the foot and leg. She fell and hurt her **ankle. ankles.**

another   She ate **another** apple. The cap didn't fit, so I chose **another.**

another

answer   **Answer** means to speak or write something when someone asks a question. He **answered** the question. **answered, answering.**

ant   An **ant** is a small insect. **Ants** live in the ground. Many **ants** live together in a group. **ants.**

ant

12

any — Choose **any** toy you like. Are there **any** cookies left?

apartment — An **apartment** is a group of rooms to live in. They live in a small **apartment** in that building. **apartments.**

apartment

ape — An **ape** is a large animal with long arms and no tail. **Apes** can stand almost straight and can walk on two feet. A gorilla is an ape. **apes.**

ape

apple — An **apple** is a fruit that grows on trees. **Apples** are red, yellow, or green. **apples.**

apple

aquarium — An **aquarium** is a place where fish and other water animals are kept. Some **aquariums** are glass bowls or boxes. Others are buildings where you can see many kinds of water animals. **aquariums.**

aquarium

13

A a

area

arm

are You **are** right. We **are** ready. They **are** waiting for us.

area The **area** of something is the amount of space it covers. A large **area** of the earth is covered by water. The dining **area** is where we eat. **areas.**

arm The **arm** is the part of the body between the shoulder and the hand. **arms.**

around

around The top spun **around.** There was a white fence **around** the yard.

art

art Paintings and drawings are kinds of **art.** The teacher showed the children's **art** to their parents.

artist

artist An **artist** is a person who makes paintings and drawings. **artists.**

as   Jane ran **as** fast **as** she could to win the race.

ask   **1.** Ask means to try to find out something. We had to **ask** the way to the monkey house.
2. Ask also means to invite someone. Tom **asked** six friends to his party. **asked, asking.**

ask

asleep   When you are **asleep** you rest your body and your mind. Jim tried to stay awake, but he fell **asleep.**

asleep

astronaut   An **astronaut** rides in a spaceship. Astronauts landed on the moon. **astronauts.**

astronaut

A | a

at

at   The boy is **at** the chalkboard. The dog barked **at** the cat.

ate   We **ate** our lunch in the park.

ate

attic

attic   An **attic** is a space in a house just below the roof. It is above the other rooms. We store things in our **attic**. **attics.**

aunt   Your **aunt** is your father's sister or your mother's sister. Your uncle's wife is also your **aunt. aunts.**

author An **author** is a person who writes books, stories, poems, or plays. Who is your favorite **author**? **authors.**

author

automobile An **automobile** is a machine that people ride in. It has a motor and four wheels. Another word for automobile is car. **automobiles.**

automobile

autumn Autumn is one of the four seasons. It comes after summer and before winter. The leaves fall from the trees in **autumn.** Another name for **autumn** is fall.

autumn

awake Awake means not asleep. We were **awake** in time to see the sun rise.

away The dog ran **away** from the bear. Jan put the game **away.** They will be **away** for a week.

awake

Bb

baby   A **baby** is a very young child. Little **babies** can't walk. **babies.**

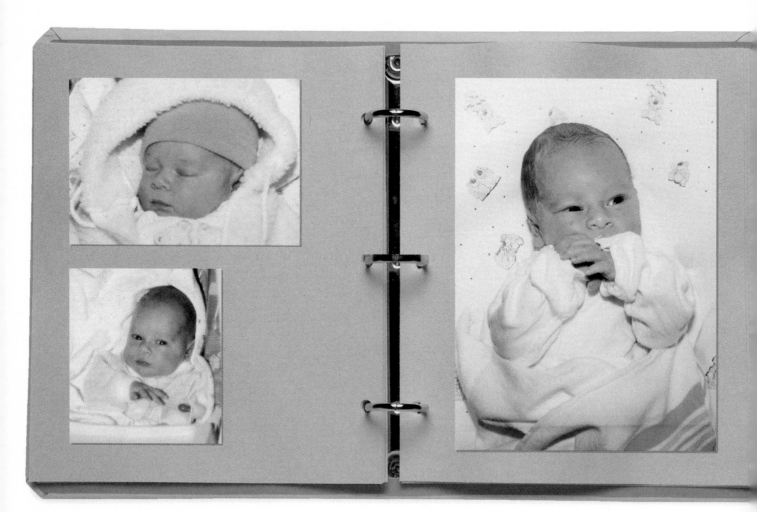

baby

back The part of the body opposite the chest and stomach is the **back**. **backs.**

back

bad **Bad** means not good or not right. That medicine tastes **bad**. That **bad** dog ate my lunch. Ann has a **bad** cold. **worse, worst.**

bad   worse   worst

bag A **bag** holds things. **Bags** can be made of paper, plastic, or other things. **bags.**

bag

bake **Bake** means to cook something in an oven. Tom helped Grandpa **bake** a cake. **baked, baking.**

baker A **baker** makes and sells bread, pies, and cakes. **bakers.**

baker

19

B b

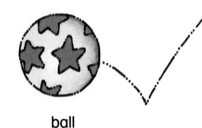

ball   A **ball** is round and is used to play games. You can throw a **ball** or bounce it. Jane kicked the **ball** to John. **balls.**

ball

balloon   A **balloon** is a toy. It is made of thin rubber filled with air. **balloons.**

banana   A **banana** is a curved, yellow fruit. Bananas grow in bunches on trees. **bananas.**

banana

bank

bank   A **bank** is a place where people keep their money. A **bank** can be a building where people work. A **bank** can be a box or jar to save pennies in. **banks.**

barber

barber   A barber is a person who cuts hair. **barbers.**

bark¹

bark¹   Bark covers the outside of a tree. It covers the trunk and branches.

20

bark² A **bark** is the sound that a dog makes. The dog's loud **bark** made me jump. **barks.**

barn

barn A **barn** is a farm building. It is used to store food for animals. Cows and horses are kept in the **barn** at night. **barns.**

baseball

baseball 1. **Baseball** is a game played with a ball and bat. 2. A **baseball** is also the name of the ball used in this game. **baseballs.**

basket A **basket** is used to hold things. A **basket** can be big or little. **baskets.**

basket

basketball 1. **Basketball** is a game played with a large ball. Players have to throw the ball through a ring. 2. A **basketball** is also the name of the ball used in this game. **basketballs.**

basketball

21

B b

bat¹   A **bat** is used to hit the ball in baseball. **bats.**

bat¹

bat²

bat²   A **bat** is a small animal that flies. Its face is like that of a mouse. Its wings are covered with skin. Bats fly around at night. **bats.**

bath   When you take a **bath** you wash your body. The baby splashes when Mom gives him a **bath**. **baths.**

bathing suit   You wear a **bathing suit** when you go swimming. **bathing suits.**

bathing suit

bathtub   A **bathtub** is a tub to take a bath in. She filled the **bathtub** with water. **bathtubs.**

bathtub

beach

B | b

be   He wants to **be** an artist when he grows up. Will Sue and Joe **be** at the party?

beach   A **beach** is an area of land next to the water. **Beaches** are covered with sand or stones. **beaches.**

bean   A **bean** is a vegetable. **Beans** grow on vines. There are string **beans**, lima **beans**, and kidney beans. **beans.**

bean

bear   A **bear** is a large animal with thick fur. Many **bears** sleep most of the winter. **bears.**

bear

beautiful

beautiful   **Beautiful** means that something we see or hear is very pretty. We saw a **beautiful** rainbow. That was a **beautiful** song.

B | b

beaver

beaver   A **beaver** is an animal with soft fur and large front teeth. It has a wide, flat tail. **Beavers** cut down trees with their teeth. They live both in water and on land. **beavers.**

became   The puppy soon **became** a big dog.

became

because   The game was called off **because** it rained.

become   This small plant will **become** a tree. It is winter, and **becoming** colder. **became, becoming.**

bed

bed   A **bed** is something to sleep on. What time do you go to **bed**? Mom put the baby in her **bed**. **beds.**

bedroom   A **bedroom** is a room to sleep in. Tom and Bob share a **bedroom**. **bedrooms.**

bedroom

bee   A **bee** is an insect that can fly. **Bees** make honey. Some **bees** live in large groups. **bees.**

bee

been   You can tell that Jan and Joe have **been** playing in the mud. Have you **been** to the circus?

beetle   A **beetle** is an insect. Its shiny front wings cover its back wings when it is not flying. **beetles.**

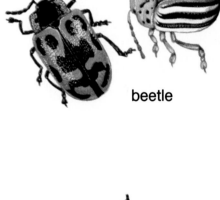

beetle

before   Your turn comes **before** mine. Have you been to the zoo **before**?

began   It **began** to snow.

begin   **Begin** means to start. When did it **begin** to snow? The race is going to begin. **began, begun, beginning.**

begin

B b

begun The wind has **begun** to blow.

behind The band marched **behind** the leader.

behind

bell

being The dog is **being** fed.

bell A **bell** makes a ringing sound. Sue rang the front door **bell**. Some **bells** make a pretty sound when you shake them. **bells.**

belong Do these mittens **belong** to you?

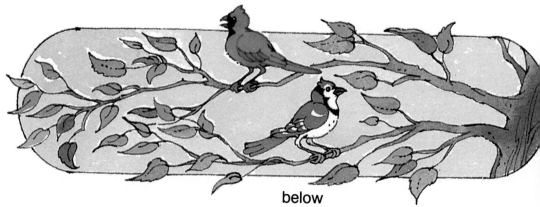

below

below The blue bird is on the branch **below** the red bird.

belt A **belt** is a strip of cloth or leather. You wear a **belt** around your waist. **belts.**

belt

bend If you **bend** something, you make it curved or crooked. The strong man said he would **bend** the piece of iron. **bent, bending.**

bent He **bent** the iron into a curve.

bent

berry A **berry** is a small, juicy fruit with seeds. Strawberries and raspberries are **berries**. **berries.**

berry

beside They camped **beside** the river. The girl was reading with her dog **beside** her.

beside

B | b

best   His work is good. Your work is better, but her work is **best**.

good   better   best

better   Sue's picture is good, but I think Pat's is **better**.

between   The boy stood **between** two tall men.

bicycle   A **bicycle** has two wheels. You ride it by pushing the pedals. **bicycles.**

between

bicycle

big   If something is **big**, it has great size. Something **big** is not little. Jerry has a **big** dog. Lita's dog is **bigger** than Jerry's. It is the **biggest** I have ever seen. **bigger, biggest.**

big   bigger

bike Bike is another word for bicycle. **bikes.**

bill A bill is part of a bird's mouth. It is hard and comes to a point. **bills.**

bill

bird A bird is an animal that has feathers, wings, and two legs. Most birds can fly. Robins, eagles, and ducks are birds. **birds.**

bird

birthday A birthday is the day on which a person is born. Birthdays can be happy days. **birthdays.**

birthday

bit He bit into the apple.

bite When you bite something, you cut it with your teeth. If you bite the apple, you should finish eating it. **bit, bitten, biting.**

bite

B | b

bitten

bitten   Someone has **bitten** this apple!

black   **Black** is a color. The words in this book are printed in **black**.

blanket

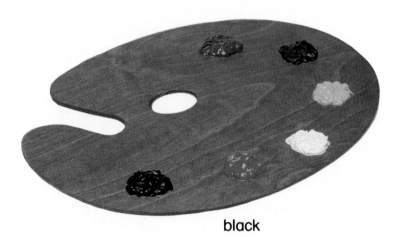
black

blanket   A **blanket** keeps you warm. Some **blankets** are soft and fluffy. I have a blue **blanket** on my bed. **blankets.**

blew   The wind **blew** the leaves all over the yard.

block   **1.** A **block** is a thick piece of wood or plastic. My little sister built a house with her blocks. **blocks.**
2. **Block** also means to fill so that nothing can pass. A big truck **blocked** the street. **blocked, blocking.**

block

blow

blow　Blow means to move air quickly. A strong wind started to **blow**. Anna helped Nan **blow** up balloons. **blew, blown, blowing.**

blown　The wind has **blown** Bob's hat off.

blue　Blue is a color. On a clear day the sky is **blue**.

blue

boat　A **boat** is something to ride in on the water. We crossed the lake in a boat. **boats.**

boat

body　Your **body** is your whole person, from head to toe. People and animals have bodies. **bodies.**

body

B | b

bone

bone A **bone** is the hard inside support that helps protect your body. **Bones** help you move. There are over 200 **bones** under your skin. **bones.**

book A **book** has sheets of paper inside two covers. The pages in this **book** have writing and pictures on them. **books.**

book

boot

boot A **boot** is a covering for the foot and leg. **Boots** keep your feet and legs dry. We wear **boots** in the rain or snow. **boots.**

bottle A **bottle** can hold milk or juice. **Bottles** are made of glass or plastic. Most **bottles** have caps on them. **bottles.**

bottle

bottom The **bottom** is the lowest part of anything. Jack held the **bottom** of the ladder as Mom climbed to the top. **bottoms.**

bought   He **bought** a new pair of shoes.

bounce   If you throw a ball against a wall it will **bounce** back to you. **Bounce** means to spring back after hitting something. **bounced, bouncing.**

bounce

bow¹   When you **bow** you bend your head or body. The actors **bowed** when the people clapped. **bowed, bowing.** Bow¹ sounds like <u>how</u>.

bow¹

bow²

bow²   A **bow** is a special kind of knot. You make a **bow** when you tie your shoe. **bows.** Bow² sounds like <u>so</u>.

bowl   A **bowl** is a deep dish. Jane ate a **bowl** of soup for lunch. **bowls.**

bowl

33

B|b

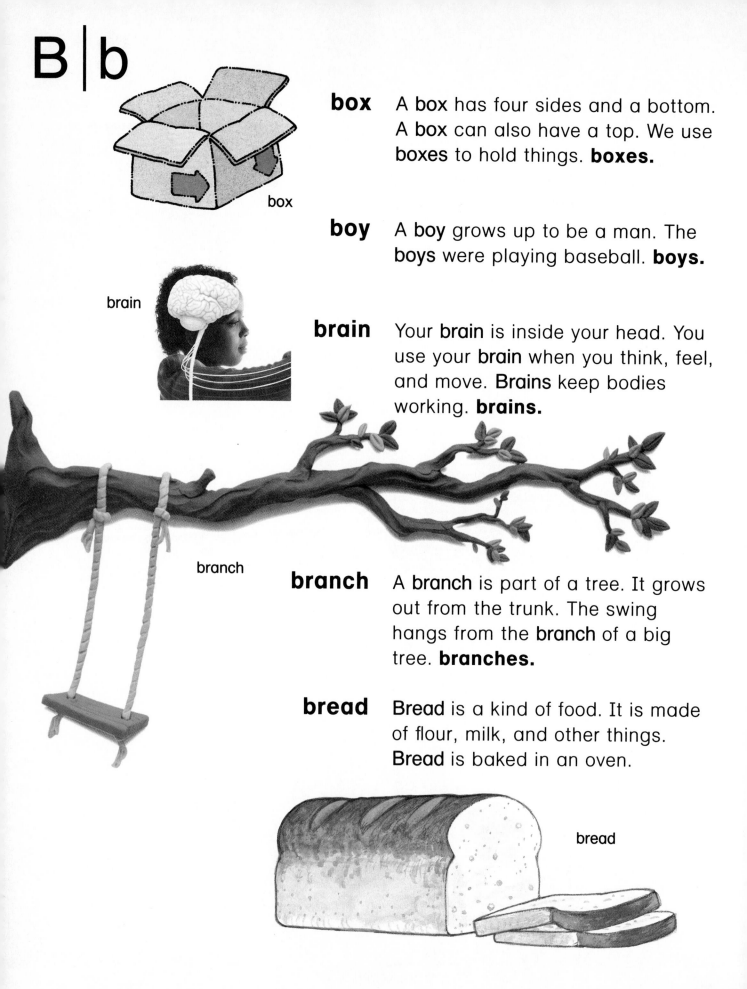

box   A **box** has four sides and a bottom. A **box** can also have a top. We use **boxes** to hold things. **boxes.**

box

boy   A **boy** grows up to be a man. The **boys** were playing baseball. **boys.**

brain

brain   Your **brain** is inside your head. You use your **brain** when you think, feel, and move. **Brains** keep bodies working. **brains.**

branch

branch   A **branch** is part of a tree. It grows out from the trunk. The swing hangs from the **branch** of a big tree. **branches.**

bread   **Bread** is a kind of food. It is made of flour, milk, and other things. **Bread** is baked in an oven.

bread

34

break   If you **break** something it comes apart or goes to pieces. You might **break** a glass bottle if you drop it. **broke, broken, breaking.**

break

breakfast   Breakfast is a meal eaten in the morning. We had cereal for **breakfast** today. **breakfasts.**

breathe   You **breathe** air through your nose or mouth. You **breathe** air in and then you **breathe** air out. **breathed, breathing.**

brick

brick   A **brick** is hard and heavy. Bricks are used to build houses and walls. **bricks.**

bridge   A **bridge** is a road built over water. We walked across the **bridge** to the other side of the river. **bridges.**

bridge

B | b

bright

bright Something that is **bright** gives much light. Something that shines is **bright.** A new penny is **bright.** The sun is **brighter** than the stars. **brighter, brightest.**

bring **Bring** means to carry something to another place. Please **bring** me a glass of water. **brought, bringing.**

broke Lee dropped the flower pot and it **broke.**

broke

broken

broom

broken He tried to fix the **broken** flower pot.

broom A **broom** is a brush with a long handle. Lee's mother used a **broom** to sweep the floor. **brooms.**

brother Your **brother** is a boy who has the same mother and father that you have. Sam has a big **brother** and a little sister. **brothers.**

brought

B|b

brought Ann's friends **brought** presents to her birthday party.

brown Brown is a color. Toast and chocolate are **brown**.

brown

brush A **brush** is made of stiff hairs or plastic. There are many kinds of **brushes**. You use a **brush** to paint a house. **brushes.**

brush

bud A **bud** is a small bump on a plant. A **bud** will grow into a flower or a leaf. **buds.**

bug A **bug** is anything that crawls or flies like an insect. A **bug** can be an ant, a fly, or a spider. **bugs.**

bug

B | b

building

burn

build   When you **build** something, you put things together. Dave can **build** a house with these blocks. **built, building.**

building   A **building** has walls and a roof. Schools, houses, and barns are **buildings.** It took many people to build that big **building. buildings.**

built   They **built** their house of brick. The fence is **built** of wood.

burn   **Burn** means to be on fire. The campfire **burned** brightly. **burned, burning.**

bus

bus   A **bus** is like a big car with many seats. A **bus** carries people from place to place. A school **bus** takes children to school. **buses.**

bush A **bush** is a plant smaller than a tree. A **bush** has branches that start near the ground. Some **bushes** have flowers, and some have fruit. **bushes.**

bush

busy When you are **busy** you have a lot to do. The children are **busy** painting a playhouse. They are the **busiest** children I've ever seen. **busier, busiest.**

but You may look at the flowers, **but** you must not pick them. We wanted to go swimming **but** we couldn't.

busy

butter Butter is a soft yellow food. It is made from cream. Tom spreads **butter** on his toast.

butter

butterfly A **butterfly** is an insect. It has two pairs of wings with bright colors. Some caterpillars change into **butterflies. butterflies.**

butterfly

B | b

button

button   A button is used to hold clothes together. Some shirts have **buttons** down the front. **buttons.**

buy   When you buy something, you pay money for it. Ruth wanted to buy a toy car. **bought, buying.**

buy

buzz   Buzz means to make a humming sound. Bees and flies buzz. **buzzed, buzzing.**

by   The playground is by the school. The tree house was built by Ann and her friends.

by

Cc

cab   A **cab** is a car with a driver. The driver is paid to take people places. **cabs.**

cactus   A **cactus** is a plant that grows in hot, dry places. Cactuses are covered with sharp points. **cactuses.**

cactus

C c

cage

cage A **cage** is a place to keep birds or wild animals. **Cages** have bars or wires. **cages.**

cake **Cake** is a sweet food made of flour, sugar, eggs, and other things. We baked a **cake** for Bob's birthday. **cakes.**

calculator

calculator A **calculator** is used to find the answers to number problems. **calculators.**

calendar

calendar A **calendar** is a kind of chart. **Calendars** show the months, weeks, and days of the year. **calendars.**

calf A **calf** is a baby cow. **calves.**

calf

call
1. Call means to shout or say something in a loud voice. He **called** to the bus driver to wait.
2. Call also means to give a name to someone or something. They **call** their dog King. **called, calling.**

calves
We saw a cow and two **calves**.

came
He **came** to the party early.

camel
A **camel** is a large animal that can carry heavy loads. **Camels** can go a long time without water. **camels.**

camel

camera
A **camera** is used to take pictures or movies. **cameras.**

camera

camp
A **camp** is a group of tents or huts where people live for a time. Many children go to summer **camps**. **camps.**

camp

43

C|c

can¹ Can you come to the party tomorrow night? She **can** sing and dance. **could.**

can²

can² A **can** is used to hold something. We buy food, paint, and fruit juice in **cans**. **cans.**

candle A **candle** is a stick of wax with a string in the center. It gives light as it burns. Kim's birthday cake had six **candles**. **candles.**

candle

candy **Candy** is a sweet food made of sugar or syrup. Chocolate, fruit, and nuts are often added to **candy**. **candies.**

candy

cannot Jean **cannot** come to the birthday party tomorrow.

44

cap   A **cap** is a kind of hat. **Caps** are soft and fit the head closely. Tom wore a blue **cap**. **caps.**

cap

capital   **1.** A **capital** is a city where a country's or state's leaders work. Washington, D.C., is the **capital** of the United States.
2. **Capital** also means A, B, C, D, or any other large letter. **capitals.**

capital

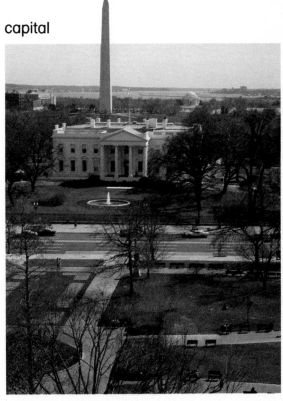

car   A **car** is a machine that people ride in. It has a motor and four wheels. Another word for **car** is automobile. **cars.**

card   A **card** is a flat piece of thick paper. A birthday **card**, a library **card**, and a report **card** are different kinds of **cards**. **cards.**

card

C c

care
1. You take **care** of someone when you look after that person. Grandmother took **care** of me.
2. Care also means to feel interest in something. He **cares** more about cars than anything else. **cared, caring.**

careful
Being **careful** means thinking about what you say or do. Be **careful** with your new bicycle.

carpenter

carpenter
A **carpenter** builds things out of wood. **Carpenters** build and fix the wooden parts of houses and boats. **carpenters.**

carrot

carrot
A **carrot** is a long, orange vegetable. **Carrots** grow under the ground. **carrots.**

carry
Carry means to take something from one place to another. Jim **carried** the bags to the kitchen. **carried, carrying.**

carry

castle   A castle is a large stone building with thick walls. Many years ago, kings and queens lived in **castles. castles.**

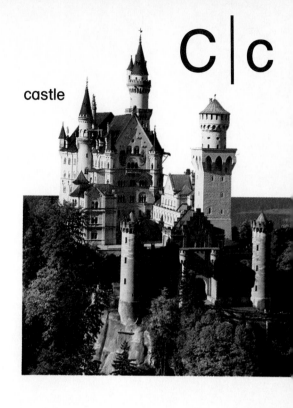
castle

cat   A cat is a small animal with soft fur. **Cats** are often kept as pets. **cats.**

cat

catch   Catch means to take and hold something moving. **Catch** the football with both hands. **caught, catching.**

caterpillar   A caterpillar is an insect. Most **caterpillars** are furry and bright in color. Some **caterpillars** change into butterflies. **caterpillars.**

caterpillar

cattle   Cattle are animals raised for milk and meat. Cows are **cattle.**

cattle

C c

caught

cave

cent

center

caught When I threw the ball, Mary **caught** it.

cause Cause means to make something happen. The fire **caused** much damage. **caused, causing.**

cave A **cave** is an empty space under the ground. Most **caves** have an opening in the side of a hill or mountain. **caves.**

cavity A **cavity** is a hole. The dentist filled two **cavities** in my teeth. **cavities.**

cent A **cent** is a kind of money. It is also called a penny. There are one hundred **cents** in a dollar. **cents.**

center Center means the middle of something. She hit the **center** of the board and won the game.

centimeter A **centimeter** is used to measure how long something is. This line is one **centimeter** long ___ . **centimeters.**

cereal **Cereal** is a food made from corn, rice, or other grains. Many people eat **cereal** with milk for breakfast. **cereals.**

cereal

chair

chair A **chair** is a seat with a back and legs. Tom sat in the **chair** by the window. **chairs.**

chalk **Chalk** is used to write or draw. The teacher used a piece of **chalk** to write her name.

chalk

change **I.** **Change** means to make something different. He **changed** the look of his bike by painting it. **changed, changing.**
2. **Change** also means money you get back. The bus driver gave me ten cents in **change.**

C|c

chart

chart A **chart** is a list or drawing that shows facts. Sara made a **chart** showing the weather each day of last week. **charts.**

check 1. **Check** means to make sure something is true or right. **Check** your answers. **checked, checking.** 2. A **check** is a mark (√) that shows something is true or right. **checks.**

cheek

cheek The **cheek** is the part of the face just below the eye. His **cheeks** are red. **cheeks.**

cheer

cheer **Cheer** means to call out or yell loudly to show you like something. Let's **cheer** for our team. **cheered, cheering.**

cheese **Cheese** is a food made from milk. We often eat **cheese** for lunch. **cheeses.**

cheese

cherry   A **cherry** is a small, red fruit. **Cherries** grow on trees and are round and juicy. **cherries.**

cherry

chest   The front part of the body between the neck and the stomach is the chest. **chests.**

chest

chew   **Chew** means to crush with the teeth. **Chew** your meat well. **chewed, chewing.**

chick

chicken

chick   A **chick** is a young chicken. **chicks.**

chicken   A **chicken** is a bird raised for food. **chickens.**

C | c

child   A child is a young boy or young girl. Children grow up to be men and women. **children.**

children

children   Children are young boys and girls.

chin   The chin is the part of the face below the mouth. **chins.**

chin

chocolate   Chocolate is a food made from the seeds of a tree. It tastes good and is used to make candy.

choose   Choose means to pick out from a group. Karen often chooses books about animals, while Sue chooses books about flying. **chose, chosen, choosing.**

choose

chose   John chose to see the movie about astronauts.

chosen Sue was **chosen** to lead the parade.

church A **church** is a place where some people go to pray. **churches.**

church

circle **1.** A **circle** is a shape like a round line. Flowers grew in a **circle** around the tree. **circles.**
2. Circle also means to go around something. He **circled** the school on his bike. **circled, circling.**

circus

circus A **circus** is a traveling show. A **circus** has clowns, horses, and wild animals. **circuses.**

city

city A **city** is a large town. Many people live and work in a **city. Cities** often have tall buildings. **cities.**

C | c

clap

clap Clap means to hit the hands together to make a sound. We **clapped** when the show was over. **clapped, clapping.**

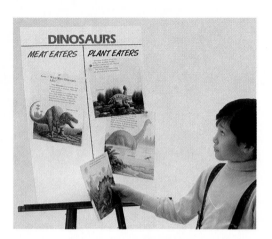
classify

class A class is a group of boys and girls who learn together. Most schools have many **classes**. **classes.**

classify Classify means to put in order by group. Jim likes to **classify** dinosaurs into meat eaters and plant eaters. **classified, classifying.**

classroom

classroom A classroom is a room in which classes are held. **classrooms.**

clay

clay Clay is a kind of earth. Wet **clay** can be shaped into pots and dishes. **Clay** gets hard when it dries.

clean

clean **1.** Clean means free from dirt. Mom is proud of her **clean** car. **cleaner, cleanest.**
2. Clean also means to make free from dirt. **Clean** your boots. **cleaned, cleaning.**

clear **1.** Clear means easy to see through. I saw my cat through the **clear** glass.
2. Clear also means bright or without clouds. On **clear** days the children went swimming. **clearer, clearest.**

clear

climb Climb means to go up something. We **climbed** the stairs. Sue **climbs** trees. **climbed, climbing.**

clock A **clock** shows what time it is. The hands of the **clock** showed it was almost noon. **clocks.**

clock

C c

close   Close means to shut. **Close** the window of your bedroom. **closed, closing.**

cloth

cloth   Cloth is used to make clothes and other things. Mom made curtains out of blue **cloth.**

clothes

clothes   Clothes cover the body. Dresses, pants, sweaters, and shirts are **clothes.**

clothing   Clothing is another word for clothes.

cloud

cloud   A **cloud** is made up of tiny drops of water. **Clouds** float high in the sky. They are white or gray. **clouds.**

clown   A **clown** is a person who makes people laugh. **Clowns** wear funny clothes and paint their faces. They do tricks and act silly. **clowns.**

clown

clue   A **clue** helps you answer a question. **Clues** helped John find the answer to the riddle. **clues.**

coal   **Coal** is found under the ground. It is black. **Coal** gives off heat when it is burned.

coat

coat   A **coat** is a piece of clothing worn over other clothes. Grace bought a new winter **coat. coats.**

cold   **1.** **Cold** means not hot. Winter weather can be **cold. colder, coldest.**
2. **Cold** also means a kind of sickness. You cough and sneeze when you have a **cold.** Many people get **colds** in the winter. **colds.**

cold

C|c

color

color **1.** Red, yellow, blue, green, orange, pink, and purple are **colors**. What **color** is Jane's new jacket? **colors.** **2. Color** also means to paint or mark with a color. Use a crayon to **color** the sky blue. **colored, coloring.**

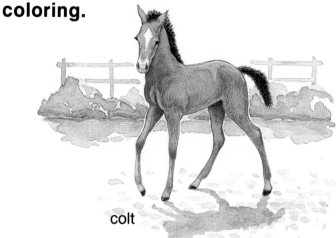

colt

colt A **colt** is a young horse or donkey. **colts.**

comb

comb A **comb** is used to keep hair neat. **combs.**

come Can you **come** to my birthday party? My dad will **come** at 6 o'clock. **came, come, coming.**

complete **1.** When something is **complete**, no parts are missing. Jim collected a **complete** set of baseball cards. **2. Complete** also means to get to the end of something. She **completed** her drawing at home. **completed, completing.**

computation   When you find something out by using mathematics, you make a **computation**. Adding 6 and 3 to get 9 is a **computation**. **computations.**

$$6+3=9$$

computation

computer   A **computer** is a machine that can keep and give back information. A **computer** can do many kinds of work. **Computers** play games and give answers to problems. **computers.**

computer

continent   A **continent** is a very large area of land. There are seven **continents** on the earth. We live on the **continent** of North America. **continents.**

cook

continent

cook   Cook means to make food ready to eat. Food **cooks** on a hot stove. John **cooked** the potatoes. **cooked, cooking.**

C c

cookie

cookie   A cookie is a small, flat cake. Kate likes to bake cookies. **cookies.**

cool   Cool means more cold than hot. The fall day was very cool. **cooler, coolest.**

copy   **I.** A copy is a thing made to be just like another. Make a copy of this page. **copies.**
2. Copy also means to make something like something else. Copy this picture. **copied, copying.**

corn

corn   Corn is a yellow or white vegetable. It grows on a tall, green plant. Animals and people eat corn.

corner

corner   A corner is the place where two lines or two sides meet. There was a chair in the corner of the room. **corners.**

correct
1. Correct means right or true. Tom had the **correct** answer.
2. Correct also means to check whether something is right or true. The teacher **corrected** my paper.
corrected, correcting.

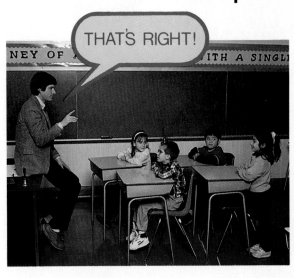
correct

cost
The amount of money needed to buy something is its **cost**. The **cost** of this record is 8 dollars. **costs.**

cost

cough
Cough means to push air out of the chest with a loud noise. She had a cold and **coughed** all night.
coughed, coughing.

cough

could
Her brother said he **could** come. When grandpa was young, he **could** dance well.

couldn't
Couldn't means could not. Her sister **couldn't** come.

C | c

count

count   **1.** Count means to name numbers in order. She can **count** to 20.
2. Count also means to add up. He counted the marbles and found there were 12. **counted, counting.**

country

country   **1.** The **country** is the land outside a city. There are many farms in the country.
2. Country also means a land and people with the same leaders. The people of a **country** usually speak the same language. There are many **countries** in the world. Our country is the United States. **countries.**

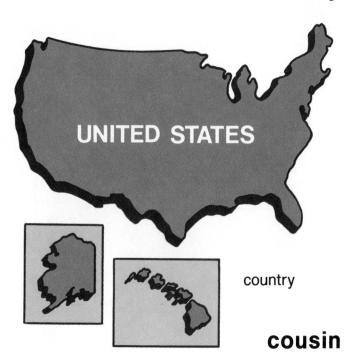

UNITED STATES

country

cousin   Your **cousin** is the son or daughter of any of your uncles or aunts. **cousins.**

cover   When you **cover** something, you put something else over it. **Cover** the baby with a blanket. **covered, covering.**

cover

cow   A **cow** is a large animal. **Cows** eat grass. We get milk from **cows**. **cows.**

cow

crayon   A **crayon** is used for drawing and coloring pictures. **Crayons** come in many colors. **crayons.**

crayon

creep   **Creep** means to move slowly with the body close to the floor. The cat was **creeping** toward the mouse. **crept, creeping.**

crept

crept   The cat **crept** without making a sound.

crib   A **crib** is a small bed with high sides. Babies sleep in **cribs**. **cribs.**

crib

crop   Plants grown by farmers for food are **crops**. Corn is an important crop. **crops.**

cross   **Cross** means to move from one side to another. Let's **cross** the street. **crossed, crossing.**

crow

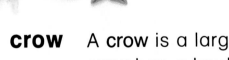

crow   A **crow** is a large, black bird. A crow has a loud cry. **crows.**

cry 1. **Cry** means to call loudly. He cried, "Look out!"
2. **Cry** also means to have tears come from the eyes. Babies **cry** when they are hungry. **cried, crying.**

cry

cup A **cup** is a dish to drink from. **Cups** are round and deep. You can drink milk from a **cup. cups.**

cup

curtain A **curtain** is a cloth hung at a window or door. Close the **curtains,** please. **curtains.**

curtain

curve A **curve** is a line with no straight part. This road has many **curves. curves.**

cut When you **cut** something, you divide it into pieces. Dad cut the meat with a knife. Juan used scissors to **cut** the paper. **cut, cutting.**

cut

65

Dd

---

dad   Dad is a short name for father.
dads.

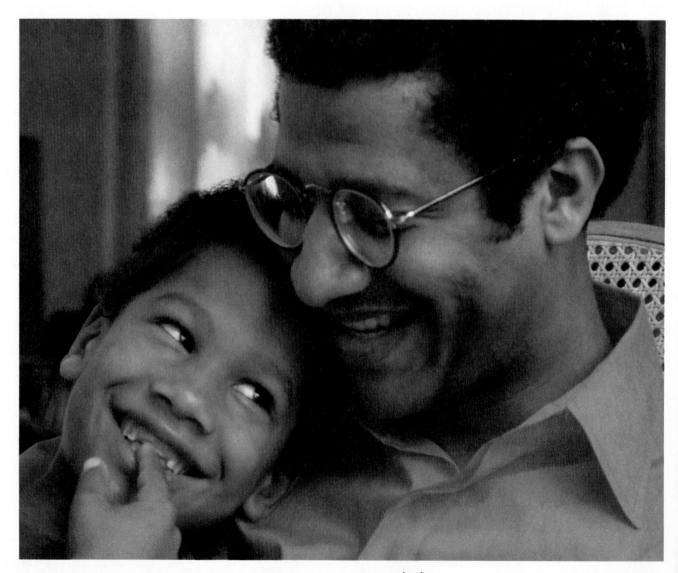

dad

daisy A **daisy** is a flower with a yellow center. **Daisies** have white, pink, or yellow petals. **daisies.**

daisy

dance

dance When you **dance**, you move to the sound of music. We **danced** at the party. **danced, dancing.**

dark When something is not light, it is **dark**. It was so **dark** I could not see. His hair is **dark**. She wore a **dark** blue sweater. **darker, darkest.**

dark

date The **date** of something is the time it happens or happened. May 4, 1982, is her birth **date**. What is the **date** today? **dates.**

daughter A **daughter** is a girl child. A girl is the **daughter** of her father and mother. The Smiths have four daughters. **daughters.**

daughter

67

D|d

day

I. Day is the time when the sun is up. **Days** are brighter and warmer than nights.

2. A **day** is also 24 hours of light and dark. There are 7 **days** in a week. **days.**

dead

When something is **dead**, it is no longer alive. No one watered the flowers, and now they are **dead**.

dead

decide

Decide means to choose or to make up your mind. Kim **decided** to eat the apple, not the cookie. **decided, deciding.**

deep

Something that is **deep** goes a long way down. I dug a **deep** hole. **deeper, deepest.**

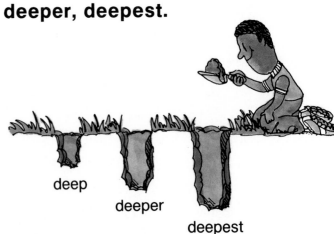

deep

deeper

deepest

deer

A **deer** is an animal that can run very fast. **deer.**

deer

dentist

dentist A dentist is a doctor who takes care of people's teeth. **dentists.**

describe To describe something is to tell about it. Kate **described** her dog so well, we could almost see it. **described, describing.**

desert

desert A desert is a place without water or trees. **Deserts** are usually hot and sandy. **deserts.**

desk A desk is where we sit in a classroom. We read and write at our desks. **desks.**

desk

dictionary A dictionary is a book that tells what words mean. People also use **dictionaries** to find out how to spell words. **dictionaries.**

did Lee **did** a good job taking care of his dog. **Did** you see Carlos today?

D | d

different Different means not alike. These hats are **different**, but these shoes are alike.

different

dig

dig Dig means to make a hole in the ground. The dog **dug** a place to hide its bone. **dug, digging.**

dime

dime A **dime** is a kind of money equal to ten cents. Ten **dimes** make one dollar. **dimes.**

dining room A dining room is a room in a house where meals are eaten. **dining rooms.**

dining room

dinner Dinner is a meal eaten in the evening. We had chicken for **dinner** last night. **dinners.**

dinosaur   A **dinosaur** is an animal that lived many years ago. **Dinosaurs** lived on the earth before there were people. Some **dinosaurs** were much bigger than elephants. Some were smaller than cats. **dinosaurs.**

dinosaur

dip   **Dip** means to put something in a liquid and quickly take it out again. She **dipped** her toe into the cold lake. **dipped, dipping.**

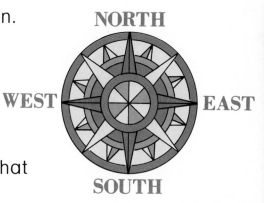

direction

direction   The **direction** of something is the way it is moving or pointing. In what **direction** are you going? North, south, east, and west are directions. **directions.**

directions   **Directions** tell you what to do or how to do something. If you follow the **directions,** you can make this toy.

directions

71

D | d

dirt   Dirt is something that is not clean. **Dirt** makes other things unclean. The children got **dirt** on their clothes when they played outside.

dirty

dirtier

dirtiest

dirty   When something is **dirty**, it is not clean. The children's boots were very **dirty**. **dirtier, dirtiest.**

dish   A **dish** is something food is placed on. We eat our meals from **dishes**. **dishes.**

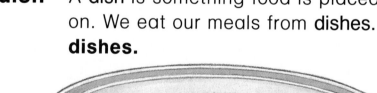
dish

distance   The **distance** between two points is the amount of space between them. What is the **distance** between New York and Chicago?

divide

divide   When you **divide** something, you break it into equal parts. Lee **divided** the apple into four parts. **divided, dividing.**

do   Do you like peanuts? I **do**! I will **do** my work tomorrow. **does, did, done, doing.**

doctor   A **doctor** is a person who helps sick people. The **doctor** gave me medicine for my cough. **doctors.**

doctor

does   **Does** she like peanuts? Yes, she **does**! He **does** all his work.

dog   A **dog** is an animal. Some **dogs** are big and some are small. Many people keep **dogs** as pets. **dogs.**

dog

doghouse   A **doghouse** is a small house for a dog. When it rains or snows, dogs go into their **doghouses**. **doghouses.**

doghouse

73

D | d

doll

donkey

door

doll   A **doll** is a toy that looks like a person. **Dolls** come in many shapes and sizes. **dolls.**

dollar

dollar   A **dollar** is a piece of paper money. It is equal to 100 cents. **dollars.**

done   She has **done** all her work. Have you **done** all your work?

donkey   A **donkey** is an animal with long ears. It looks like a little horse. **donkeys.**

don't   **Don't** means do not. **Don't** forget your books. I **don't** want to go out in the rain.

door   You open a **door** to go into a building or room. Cars also have **doors**. Some **doors** can be locked. **doors.**

74

dot   A **dot** is a tiny, round mark. Put a **dot** over each "i" you write. My new shorts have red **dots** on them. **dots.**

dot

dove   A **dove** is a large bird with short legs. **doves.**

down   When something goes **down,** it goes from a higher place to a lower place. The pony ran **down** the hill. I sat **down.**

dove

dragon

dragon   A **dragon** is a large animal that breathes fire. **Dragons** are make-believe animals. Many old stories tell about **dragons.** They can fly and often fight with people. **dragons.**

drank   Pat **drank** four glasses of milk.

D | d

draw

draw When you **draw**, you make a picture. You can **draw** with pencils, crayons, chalk, or pens. **drew, drawn, drawing.**

drawn I have **drawn** a picture of my cat.

dream A **dream** is something that seems to happen while you sleep. **Dreams** can be good or bad. Bob had a **dream** about playing baseball. **dreams.**

dream

dress

dress 1. A **dress** is something a girl or woman wears. **Dresses** are a kind of clothing. **dresses.**
2. When you **dress**, you put on your clothes. May is **dressing** for school. **dressed, dressing.**

drew She **drew** a pretty picture.

drink   Drink means to swallow water, milk, or some other liquid. I **drank** a glass of milk. **drank, drunk, drinking.**

drink

drive   Drive means to make a car go. My brother can **drive**. He is **driving** me to school today. **drove, driven, driving.**

driven   He has **driven** me home many times.

driver

driver   A person who drives a car is a driver. **drivers.**

drop   Drop means to let something fall. Chris **dropped** some of the plates. **dropped, dropping.**

drop

drove   My mother **drove** me to school.

D | d

drum

dug

drum A **drum** makes a sound when it is hit. **Drums** are often hit with sticks. **drums.**

drunk I have **drunk** four glasses of milk today.

dry

dry When something has no water in it, it is **dry**. Kate's hair is **dry**, but Lee's is wet. **drier, driest.**

duck A **duck** is a bird with short legs. **Ducks** live near lakes and rivers. They like to swim. **ducks.**

duck

dug My dog **dug** a hole in the yard.

dump **Dump** means to throw down. The girls **dumped** all their toys on the floor. **dumped, dumping.**

Ee

each   Each child gets a balloon.

eagle   An **eagle** is a large bird with long wings. **Eagles** can see things from a great distance. **eagles.**

eagle

E|e

ear

ear The **ear** is the part of the body that helps you hear. Your **ears** are on each side of your head. **ears.**

early **Early** means before the usual time. Let's get up **early** in the morning to take a walk. **earlier, earliest.**

earth

earth The **earth** is the whole world. All the people and animals live on the **earth.**

east

east **East** is a direction. The sun comes up in the **east. East** is the opposite direction to west.

easy **Easy** means not hard to do or understand. That was an **easy** question to answer. **easier, easiest.**

eat **1.** Eat means to chew and swallow food. Cows **eat** grass.
2. Eat also means to have a meal. Let's **eat.** We will **eat** at Amy's house. **ate, eaten, eating.**

eaten Bob has **eaten** dinner already.

eat

edge Edge means the place where something ends. Her glass was too close to the **edge** of the table. **edges.**

edge

effect An **effect** is what happens because of something else. One **effect** of the heavy rain was water in the streets. **effects.**

egg

egg An **egg** is a food. **Eggs** are laid by chickens and are often eaten at breakfast. Other animals also lay eggs. **eggs.**

elbow The part of the arm that can bend is the **elbow. elbows.**

elbow

E | e

electric light

electricity

Electricity is a kind of energy that makes light and heat. **Electricity** makes televisions, radios, and other machines work.

electric light

An **electric light** is a light that works by electricity. We use **electric lights** after it gets dark. **electric lights.**

elephant

An **elephant** is the largest four-footed animal. It has large ears and a long trunk. **elephants.**

elephant

elevator

elevator

An **elevator** is like a small room that moves up and down. **Elevators** carry people up and down in buildings. **elevators.**

elf

An **elf** is a tiny make-believe person in a story. **Elves** are full of tricks. **elves.**

elf

else   Will someone **else** go in my place?
Let's go somewhere **else** for lunch.

elves   Fairy tales often tell about **elves.**

empty   When something is **empty**, there is nothing in it. The glass is **empty.**

empty

elves

end   **End** means the last part of something. Don is at the **end** of the line. Did you read the **end** of the story? **ends.**

end

energy   **Energy** makes people and things able to work and move. People get **energy** from food. Electricity is a form of **energy.**

enough   There is **enough** food for everyone. Have you eaten **enough?**

E | e

equal

equal **1.** Equal means the same. The two dogs are **equal** in size.
2. Equal also means to be the same as something else. Five pennies **equal** one nickel. **equaled, equaling.**

even

estimate Estimate means to make a guess. She **estimated** it would take one hour to do the work. **estimated, estimating.**

even **1.** Even means flat and smooth. The ground here is **even**.
2. Even also means at the same height. The snow is **even** with the window.

evening Evening is the time between sunset and going to bed. It gets dark in the **evening**. **evenings.**

ever Do you **ever** go swimming?

evening

84

every   **Every** child loves to play. Read **every** word.

everyone   **Everyone** must bring a book to class.

exercise

exercise   **1. Exercise** means to move the body to improve health. You **exercise** when you run, swim, or play ball. The runner **exercises** every day. **exercised, exercising. 2.** An **exercise** is something that gives practice. Read the page and then do the **exercise. exercises.**

explain   **Explain** means to tell about something so people are able to understand. She will **explain** how to play the game. **explained, explaining.**

eye

eye   The **eye** is the part of the body that helps you see. Your eyes are in your face. **Eyes** can be brown, blue, green, gray, and some other colors. **eyes.**

Ff

fable   A **fable** is a story that teaches a lesson. Many **fables** are about talking animals. **fables.**

fable

F | f

face   The front part of the head is the **face**. Your eyes, nose, and mouth are part of your **face**. Everyone's **face** is different. **faces.**

face

fact   A **fact** is something that is known to be true. It is a **fact** that Thanksgiving is a holiday. **facts.**

factory

factory   People make things at a **factory**. TV sets are made in **factories**. **factories.**

fair¹   **Fair** means going by the rules. If you are not **fair**, no one will want to play with you. **fairer, fairest.**

fair²

fair²   A **fair** is an outdoor show that is fun to see. **Fairs** have farm animals and other things. They often have rides and games. **fairs.**

F | f

fairy In stories, a **fairy** is a tiny, make-believe person. **Fairies** can do unusual things. **fairies.**

fairy

fall **1.** Fall means to drop down from a higher place. She **fell** off the branch of the tree. **fell, fallen, falling.**
2. Fall is one of the four seasons. It comes after summer and before winter. The trees lose their leaves in the **fall.** Another name for **fall** is autumn.

fall

fallen The leaves have **fallen** from the tree.

fallen

family A mother, a father, and their children make up a **family.** Family also means cousins, aunts, uncles, and grandparents. **families.**

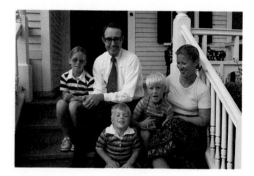

family

fan A **fan** is a machine that blows the air around. **Fans** keep people cool in hot weather. **fans.**

fan

far   Far means a long way. Our house is **far** from the ocean. **farther, farthest.**

farm   A farm is the land on which a farmer grows food and raises animals. **farms.**

farm

farmer

farmer   A farmer is a person who works on a farm. Some **farmers** grow corn. Some **farmers** raise chickens. **farmers.**

farther

farther   I jumped **farther** than you did.

farthest   Beth jumped the **farthest** of all.

farthest

fast   **1. Fast** means quick. She is a **fast** runner.
2. When you go **fast**, you go in a quick way. Some boats go very **fast**. **faster, fastest.**

fast

F | f

fat Fat means weighing more than usual. That **fat** dog needs exercise. **fatter, fattest.**

fat

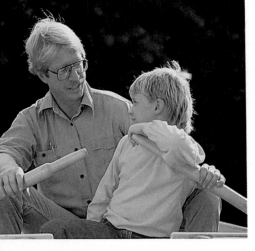

father

father A father is a man who has a child or children. **Fathers** and mothers are parents. **fathers.**

favorite Your **favorite** sport is the sport you like best. Swimming is Jack's **favorite** sport.

feather

feather A feather is part of a bird's body. **Feathers** are soft and light. **feathers.**

fed Susan **fed** the baby.

feed **Feed** means to give food to someone. It's time to **feed** the baby. Adam **fed** the dog. **fed, feeding.**

feed

feel

feel　**1.** Feel means to touch something. Sam likes to **feel** the soft fur of his cat.
2. When you **feel** sad, you are sad in your mind. When you **feel** happy you are happy in your mind. **felt, feeling.**

feeling

feeling　A **feeling** is the way you feel about something in your mind. Sadness and love are **feelings. feelings.**

feet　People have two **feet**, but dogs have four **feet**.

feet

fell　The child **fell** off the bicycle.

felt　Susan **felt** the mud between her toes.

fell

91

F f

fence A **fence** around a garden or yard keeps animals out. A **fence** also shows where someone's yard ends. **fences.**

fence

few When there are **few** people, there are not many people. There are a **few** peanuts in the bowl. **fewer, fewest.**

few

field A **field** is a piece of land without trees. Some kinds of **fields** are football **fields** and corn **fields**. **fields.**

field

fight People **fight** when they are angry. The kids are **fighting** over the ball. They **fight** every time they play ball. **fought, fighting.**

fight

fill Fill means to make something so full that there is no more room. Mr. Jones is **filling** a glass with fruit juice. Jenny **filled** the bowl with apples. **filled, filling.**

fill

find Find means to come upon something. Danny **finds** lots of shells. Did you **find** my gloves? **found, finding.**

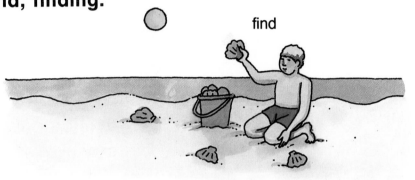

find

fine Fine means very good. He painted a **fine** picture. It was a **fine** day. **finer, finest.**

finger A finger is a part of the hand. Each hand has five **fingers.** You can pick up things with your **fingers. fingers.**

finger

finish Finish means to get to the end of something. **Finish** your work before you go out. **finished, finishing.**

fire When something burns, it causes a fire. **Fires** are hot and can cause harm. Water can put out most **fires. fires.**

fire

F f

firefighter   A **firefighter** is a person whose work is putting out fires. **Firefighters** ride on fire trucks. **firefighters.**

firefighter

first   **First** means coming before all others. The **first** letter of the alphabet is A. Ann sang **first.**

first

fish   A **fish** is an animal that lives in the water. There are many kinds of **fish.** Some kinds live in the ocean. Some live in lakes and rivers. **fish.**

fish

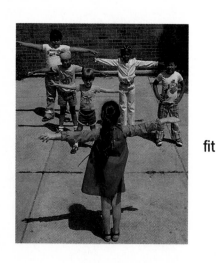

fit

fit   **1.** **Fit** means healthy and strong. Exercise will help to keep your body fit. **fitter, fittest.**
2. **Fit** also means to have the right size or shape. Do the shoes **fit**? **fitted, fitting.**

fix

fix   When you **fix** something broken, you make it work again. Dad and I fixed my bicycle. **fixed, fixing.**

flag   A **flag** is a piece of colored cloth with stars or other shapes on it. Every country has its own **flag**. The **flag** of the United States is red, white, and blue. **flags.**

flag

flashlight   A **flashlight** is a small light you can carry. It helps you see in the dark. **flashlights.**

flashlight

flat   **Flat** means smooth and even. A table has a **flat** top. A football field should be flat. **flatter, flattest.**

flew   The eagle **flew** over the hill.

float   **Float** means to move slowly on top of the water or in the air. It's fun to **float** in a pool. The red balloon **floated** in the sky. **floated, floating.**

float

F f

floor

floor

floor   **I.** A **floor** is the part of a room you walk on. He cleaned the **floor** of his room.
2. Floor can also mean one of the stories of a building. Susan lives on the fifth **floor. floors.**

floss   Floss means to use a special thread to clean between the teeth. I **flossed** my teeth last night. **flossed, flossing.**

flow

flow   Flow means to move like water in a stream. The river **flows** past the town. **flowed, flowing.**

flower

flower   A **flower** is a part of a plant. **Flowers** are pretty and come in many colors. Many **flowers** smell nice. Roses and tulips are **flowers. flowers.**

flown   Have you ever **flown** in an airplane?

F | f

fly¹ A **fly** is an insect with two wings. There are many kinds of **flies. flies.**

fly¹

fly² **1.** Fly means to move through the air with wings. Some birds **fly** south for the winter.
2. Fly also means to travel by airplane. We will **fly** to the Rocky Mountains next summer. **flew, flown, flying.**

fly²

foam Foam is made up of very small bubbles. The **foam** on the soft drink spilled over the top of the glass.

foam

fold

fold Fold means to bend or turn part of a thing over another part. Please help me **fold** the napkins. **folded, folding.**

folk tale A folk tale is an old story that has been told for many years by many people. **folk tales.**

follow Follow means to go after or come after. The dog **followed** me home. Night **follows** day. **followed, following.**

follow

97

F | f

food Food is what you eat. **Food** helps people grow and gives them energy. Fruit, vegetables, and meats are **food. foods.**

food

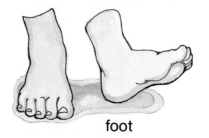

foot

foot The **foot** is the part of the body at the end of the leg. People walk on their two **feet. feet.**

football

football Football is a game played on a field. One team tries to kick, throw, or carry the football down the field. The other team tries to stop the first team.

for She went to the store **for** milk. We went **for** a swim. This orange is **for** you.

forest A forest is a place with thick woods. Many animals live in the forest. **forests.**

forest

forget   Forget means to be unable to remember. Don't **forget** your lunch, Tim. **forgot, forgotten, forgetting.**

forgot   Tim **forgot** to bring his lunch.

forgotten   Tim has **forgotten** his lunch many times.

forget

fork   A **fork** has sharp points and is used to eat with. You lift food from a dish to your mouth with a **fork**. **forks.**

fork

fought   He **fought** with me today.

found   She **found** a dime on the road.

found

fox

fox   A **fox** is an animal about the size of a small dog. It has a pointed nose and thick fur. **foxes.**

F | f

fraction

Cut an apple into equal parts. Each part is a **fraction** of the whole thing. Cut a pear into two equal parts. Each part is equal to the fraction 1/2. **fractions.**

fraction

free

free

1. **Free** means loose, or not shut up. She set the bird **free** from the cage.

2. When something is **free**, you do not have to pay money for it. The show in the park is **free**.

freeze

freeze

When something **freezes**, it becomes very cold and hard. Water turns into ice when it **freezes**. **froze, frozen, freezing.**

fresh

1. **Fresh** means just made or grown. I would like some of that **fresh** bread. **Fresh** tomatoes are good to eat. **fresher, freshest.**

2. When water is **fresh**, it has no salt in it. Rivers and lakes have **fresh** water. People like to drink **fresh** water.

fresh

F | f

friend A **friend** is someone you like and who likes you. It is nice to have friends. **friends.**

frog A **frog** is a small animal with long back legs. **Frogs** jump from place to place. Most **frogs** live near water. **frogs.**

friend

frog

from Is Mary home **from** school? Billy took a book **from** the table. Three weeks **from** today is David's birthday.

front **Front** means the part of anything that faces forward. You see the **front** of our house from the street.

front

froze It was so cold the pond **froze**.

frozen Ice is water that has **frozen**.

frozen

fruit A **fruit** is the part of a tree, bush, or vine that has seeds in it. **Fruit** is good to eat. Apples, oranges, grapes, and strawberries are different kinds of **fruit**.

fruit

F | f

fry Fry means to cook in hot fat. He loves to eat **fried** chicken for dinner. **fried, frying.**

full Full means not able to hold more. The bag is **full. fuller, fullest.**

full

fun

funny

fun When you have **fun**, you have a good time. The children had **fun** on the swing.

funny When something is **funny**, it makes you laugh. The children laughed at the **funny** clown. **funnier, funniest.**

fur

fur Fur is hair that is thick and soft. It covers the skin of many animals. Some bears have white **fur.**

G g

game   A game is something you can play.
Children like to play games.
games.

game

G | g

garage

garage A **garage** is a place where cars are parked or fixed. Mechanics fix cars in **garages**. My father parks his car in the garage. **garages.**

garden A **garden** is a place where vegetables or flowers are grown. There are roses in our **garden**. **gardens.**

garden

gas **I.** A **gas** is something that is not liquid or solid. A **gas** has no special size or shape. Air is made up of **gases**. Most **gases** have no color and cannot be seen. **gases.**
2. Gas also means a liquid that is put into cars and other machines to make them go. Our car stopped because it was out of **gas**.

gas

gate A **gate** is a door in a fence or wall. Be sure to close the **gate**. **gates.**

gate

gave Bob **gave** his mother a flower.

geese **Geese** means more than one goose. The **geese** swam on the lake.

geese

germ A **germ** is a very tiny animal or plant. **Germs** can be seen only with a microscope. Some **germs** cause people to get sick. **germs.**

get Sam hopes to **get** presents on his birthday. When I **get** home, I eat a snack. Mom **gets** up early. **got, gotten, getting.**

ghost In stories, a **ghost** is a white shape that scares people. **Ghosts** are not real. **ghosts.**

ghost

giant

giant In stories, a **giant** is a person of very large size. **Giants** are very strong. **giants.**

G | g

giraffe

giraffe   A **giraffe** is a very tall animal. It has spots on its skin, and has a very long neck. **giraffes.**

girl   A **girl** grows up to be a woman. The **girls** were playing baseball. **girls.**

give

give   **Give** means to hand over something. Mother is **giving** me a birthday present. **Give** me that pencil. **gave, given, giving.**

given   Were you **given** a glass of juice?

glad

glad   **Glad** means happy. We were **glad** to see Dad. **gladder, gladdest.**

glass 1. **Glass** is used for windows and many other things. You can see through **glass**. It is hard, but easy to break.
2. A **glass** is something to drink from. You can drink water or milk from a **glass**. **glasses.**

glass

globe A **globe** is a small copy of the earth. A **globe** is round and has a map of the earth drawn on it. Can you find the United States on the globe? **globes.**

globe

glossary A **glossary** is a list of hard words with their meanings. There is a **glossary** at the end of the book. **glossaries.**

glove

glove A **glove** covers your hand. **Gloves** keep your hands warm. **gloves.**

glue **Glue** is something used to stick things together. He used **glue** to fix the broken toy.

glue

G | g

go   Go means to move from one place to another. Roger likes to **go** to the store. He **goes** there every day. That car is **going** fast. **went, gone, going.**

goat

goat   A **goat** is an animal with horns. **Goats** have hair under their chins. **goats.**

goldfish

goldfish   A **goldfish** is a small, orange fish. Many people keep **goldfish** in glass bowls. **goldfish.**

gone   They have **gone** to a movie.

good   When something is **good**, it is right and as it ought to be. If something is **good**, it is not bad. Dad said my drawing was **good**. Rover is a **good** dog. That was a **good** story. **better, best.**

good   better   best

good-by   Good-by is something people say when they are going away. People also say **good-by** when they finish talking on the telephone. Ann said **good-by** as she was leaving. **good-bys.**

good-by

goose

goose   A **goose** is a large bird with a long neck. **Geese** like to swim. **geese.**

gorilla   A gorilla is a very large ape. Gorillas have long arms. **gorillas.**

gorilla

got   She **got** ice skates for her birthday.

gotten   He has **gotten** tired of waiting.

got

G g

grade   A **grade** is a year of study in school. She is in the first **grade**. **grades.**

grandfather   A **grandfather** is the father of your mother or father. **grandfathers.**

grandma   **Grandma** means grandmother. **grandmas.**

grandfather

grandmother

grandmother   A **grandmother** is the mother of your father or mother. **grandmothers.**

grandpa   **Grandpa** means grandfather. **grandpas.**

grape

grape   A **grape** is a small, round fruit. **Grapes** grow on vines. They may be red, purple, or green. **grapes.**

graph A **graph** is a line or drawing showing information. You could draw a **graph** to show how your weight has changed over the years. **graphs.**

graph

grass

grass **Grass** is a plant. It is green and grows in fields, parks, and yards. Horses, cows, and sheep eat **grass**.

gray **Gray** is a color. A hippopotamus is **gray**. Clouds are **gray** before a storm.

great **1. Great** means very big or large. There was a **great** crowd at the picnic.
2. Great also means very good. That's a **great** idea you have. **greater, greatest.**

gray

great

G g

green

green Green is a color. Grass and leaves are **green** in the summer.

greeting

greeting A greeting is something you say or do when you meet someone. "Hello" is a **greeting**. **greetings.**

grew She **grew** two inches this year.

grocery

grocery A grocery is a store that sells food. **groceries.**

ground

ground Ground means the soil or dirt on the earth. We planted flowers in the ground.

group

group A group is a number of persons or things together. One **group** of children played ball, and another **group** jumped rope. **groups.**

grow   Grow means to get bigger. Children grow every year. The sunflower is growing fast. **grew, grown, growing.**

grow

grown   The sunflower has **grown** every day.

grown-up   A grown-up is a person who has finished growing. **Grown-ups** are adults. **grown-ups.**

grown-up

guess   Guess means to try to find the answer to something. When you **guess** you are not sure. He **guessed** there would be ten children at the party. **guessed, guessing.**

guitar

guitar   A guitar makes music. You play a **guitar** with your fingers. He played a song on his **guitar. guitars.**

Hh

had   Pat **had** a cold. He **had** to stay in bed.

hair   Hair grows on your head. **Hair** can be brown, black, yellow, red, white, or gray. **hairs.**

hair

half A **half** is one of two equal parts. I cut my apple in **half** and shared it with Eric. Kay ate **half** a sandwich. **halves.**

halves

halves **Halves** are more than one half. Two **halves** make a whole.

ham

ham **Ham** is meat from a hog. Liz ate a **ham** sandwich. **hams.**

hamburger **Hamburger** is meat from a cow. **Hamburgers** are cooked in a round, flat shape. They are often eaten in a sandwich. **hamburgers.**

hamburger

hammer

hammer A **hammer** is a tool used for hitting nails. **hammers.**

hamster

hamster A **hamster** is an animal that looks like a mouse. Some people keep hamsters as pets. **hamsters.**

H|h

hand **1.** The **hand** is the part of the body at the end of the arm. People can hold things in their **hands**.
2. A **hand** is also part of a clock. Clock **hands** show the hours and the minutes in a day. **hands.**

hand

hang

hang To **hang** means to be held from above. Kay can **hang** by her knees. Please **hang** up your coat. **hung, hanging.**

happen Happen means to take place. What happened at the party? **happened, happening.**

happy

happy When you are **happy**, you feel good about things. Amy was **happy** to see her friend. **happier, happiest.**

hard

hard
1. Something that is **hard** is solid, not soft. The red chair is soft, but the wooden chair is **hard**.
2. Hard also means taking a lot of work or energy. When something is **hard** it is not easy. Washing the car was a **hard** job. **harder, hardest.**

harm
Harm is something that hurts or causes pain. If you follow the safety rules, you should come to no **harm.**

has

has
Pat still **has** a cold. He **has** to stay in bed. Kate **has** a new dog.

hat

hat
A **hat** is something you wear on your head. **hats.**

have
Pat and I both **have** colds. We **have** to stay in bed. The Burkes **have** a new TV. **has, had, having.**

have

H|h

hay   Hay is special food for horses and cows. It is made up of dried plants and grass.

hay

haystack

haystack   A haystack is a large amount of hay stored outside. **haystacks.**

he

he   Who is **he**? **He** is my friend, Lee. **He** likes to sing.

head

head   The **head** is the top part of your body, above the neck. Your brain, eyes, nose, mouth, and ears are in your **head. heads.**

health   Health means being well, not sick. Good food, sleep, and exercise are important to your **health.**

healthy

healthy   Healthy means to be in good health. Prince is a very **healthy** dog. **healthier, healthiest.**

hear   We **hear** by taking in sounds through our ears. I **hear** a knock at the door. Prince **heard** the sound too. **heard, hearing.**

hear

heard   When Prince **heard** the sound, he began to bark.

heard

hearing   **Hearing** is the sense that lets us take in sounds through our ears. My dog's **hearing** is very good.

heart   The **heart** is a part of the body. Your **heart** is inside your chest. When you run, your **heart** beats fast. **hearts.**

heart

heat   **Heat** means to make something warm or hot. Sue **heated** soup on the stove. **heated, heating.**

heat

H|h

heavy

heel

heavy When something is **heavy**, it weighs very much. An elephant is **heavy**, but a rabbit is light. **heavier, heaviest.**

heel The **heel** is the back part of the foot. **heels.**

held The father **held** his baby in his arms.

helicopter

helicopter A **helicopter** is a machine that flies. Helicopters can fly straight up in the air. **helicopters.**

hello When you meet someone, you say **hello**. Jenny said **hello** to me.

hello

hello!

help When you **help** someone, you do something useful for them. Tom **helped** his mother wash the car. **helped, helping.**

helper A **helper** is someone who helps others. Tom is a good **helper**. **helpers.**

hen A **hen** is a chicken that lays eggs. **hens.**

hen

her I like **her**. I do not like **her** dog. Give **her** the book.

her

here Please come **here**. **Here** is your present.

hid

hid The kitten **hid** behind a tree. She **hid** from the big dog.

hidden The kitten was well **hidden** from the dog.

H | h

high

hide   **Hide** means to try to keep out of sight. My kitten always **hides** from the big dog. **hid, hidden, hiding.**

high   When something is **high**, it is up above the ground. The kite is too **high** for Sam to reach. Kate can jump **high**. **higher, highest.**

hill   A **hill** is a high piece of ground. **Hills** are smaller than mountains. **hills.**

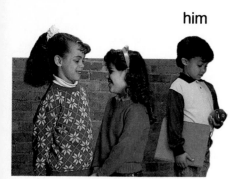

him

him   I like **him**. I gave **him** my apple. When did you give it to **him**?

hippopotamus

hippopotamus   A **hippopotamus** is a very large animal. **Hippopotamuses** have thick skin without hair. They live near rivers. **hippopotamuses.**

his

his   **His** name is Marco. This is **his** dog. My dog is young, but **his** is old.

hit Hit means to push hard against something. Jenny **hit** the ball with her bat. Bob **hit** his brother in the arm. **hit, hitting.**

hit

hog

hog A **hog** is a pig raised for food. **hogs.**

hold **1.** To **hold** something is to take it in your hands or arms. Please **hold** my coat. Nick **held** the baby.
2. **Hold** also means to have space for something. This big glass **holds** a lot of water. **held, holding.**

hold

hole A **hole** is an empty space in something. I dug a **hole** in the ground. There is a **hole** in my sweater. **holes.**

hole

holiday A **holiday** is a special day. People do not work or go to school on **holidays**. Thanksgiving is a **holiday**. **holidays.**

123

H | h

honey

home   Your **home** is the place where you live. Gail's **home** is on Oak Street. **homes.**

honey   Honey is the sweet liquid made by bees. **Honey** tastes good on bread.

hook   A **hook** is something to hang things on. Sam hung his hat on a **hook**. **hooks.**

hook

hop

hop   Hop means to jump. The rabbit **hopped** away. Jane **hops** on one foot. **hopped, hopping.**

hope   Hope means to want something to happen. I **hope** you are well soon. **hoped, hoping.**

horn

horn   **1.** A **horn** makes music when you blow into it.
2. A **horn** is also a hard, pointed part of an animal's head. Cattle and goats have **horns**. **horns.**

horn

horn

horse   A **horse** is a large animal. **Horses** can run fast. Many people like to ride **horses**. **horses.**

horse

hose   A **hose** is a long tube used to carry water. Lee brought the **hose** to water the flowers. **hoses.**

hospital   A **hospital** is a place where sick people go. The doctors and nurses in the **hospital** help these people. **hospitals.**

hospital

hot   When something is **hot**, it is very, very warm. A sunny day in August can be **hot**. Fire is **hot**. Do not touch the **hot** stove. **hotter, hottest.**

hot

hot dog

hot dog   A **hot dog** is a food made of meat. It has a long, round shape. We ate **hot dogs** on rolls at the picnic. **hot dogs.**

H|h

hour

hug

hotel A **hotel** is a place where people can stay when they are traveling. **Hotels** have many rooms. **hotels.**

hour An **hour** is used to measure time. There are 60 minutes in one **hour.** Twenty-four **hours** make one day. **hours.**

house A **house** is a building where people live. Mary's **house** is in the city. Nick's **house** is in the country. **houses.**

house

how How is Jim today? **How** far away do you live? **How** did this happen?

hug Hug means to hold someone in your arms. Meg **hugged** her mom. **hugged, hugging.**

hum Hum means to make a singing sound with the lips closed. Kelly **hummed** as she wrote. **hummed, humming.**

H|h

human

human When something is **human**, it is about people. A **human** body is the body of a person. All people are **human** beings.

hummingbird A **hummingbird** is a very small bird. **Hummingbirds** have long bills and narrow wings that move very fast. **hummingbirds.**

hummingbird

hung Sam **hung** his hat on the hook. Jenny **hung** by her knees.

hungry When you are **hungry**, you feel the need to eat. Kay was so **hungry** she ate a sandwich and a pear. **hungrier, hungriest.**

hungry

hurry Hurry means to go very quickly. I had to **hurry** because I was late. **hurried, hurrying.**

OW!

hurt Hurt means to be in pain. Mike's foot **hurts**. He **hurt** his foot on a rock. **hurt, hurting.**

hurt

I i

I   I watched television last night.

ice   Ice is frozen water. In winter there is **ice** on the pond. She put two pieces of **ice** in her lemonade.

ice

I | **i**

ice cream

ice cream   Ice cream is a frozen food. It is sweet. Let's have **ice cream** after dinner.

ice skate

ice skate   An ice skate is a kind of shoe with a piece of metal on the bottom for skating on ice. **ice skates.**

idea

idea   An idea is a thought or plan. It was my **idea** to sell lemonade. **ideas.**

if   You can come if you want to. Let's see if Ann wants to come.

iguana

iguana   An iguana is a large lizard that lives in warm places. **Iguanas** like to swim. **iguanas.**

I i

I'm   I'm means I am. I'm going to the circus tomorrow.

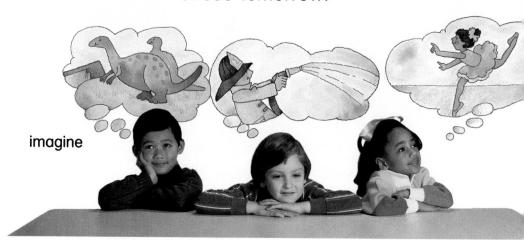

imagine

imagine   Imagine means to make a picture of something in the mind. Can you imagine a world of dinosaurs? **imagined, imagining.**

important

important   **1.** Important means having great meaning. Your birthday is an important day.
2. Important also means well-known. A king is an important person.

in

in   The white cat is in the house, and the black cat is out. It is cold here in winter. Be home in time for lunch. Please come in.

inch

inch   An inch is used to measure how long something is. A ruler shows how long an inch is. **inches.**

information   Information means facts that are known. James has a lot of information about dogs.

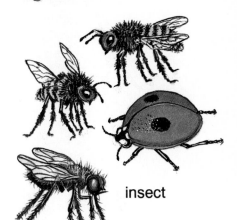

information

insect   An insect is any small animal with six legs. Insects have wings, and their bodies are divided into three parts. Flies and bees are insects. **insects.**

insect

inside   The inside of our house needs painting. There are people inside the store. John stayed inside because it was raining.

inside

into   Come into the house. It was so cold the water turned into ice.

invite   Invite means to ask someone to come to some place or to do something. Gail invited us to her party. **invited, inviting.**

invite

131

I i

iron

iron Iron means to make clothes smooth. Mother **ironed** four dresses after work. **ironed, ironing.**

is Her dog **is** outside. **Is** it starting to rain?

island An **island** is land with water all around it. There are many **islands** in the ocean. **islands.**

island

it It is nine o'clock in the morning. Is it too early to telephone Jack? My ball is at his house and I need **it**.

its The dog hid **its** bone under my bed.

its

132

Jj

jacket A jacket is a kind of short coat.
Boys and girls wear **jackets** in cool
weather. **jackets.**

jacket

J | j

jacks   Jacks is a game played with a ball and small, hard pieces. The pieces are picked up as the ball is bounced.

jacks

jar   A jar is used to hold things. **Jars** look like wide bottles. Some **jars** are made of glass. Peanut butter comes in a jar. **jars.**

jar

jeans   Jeans are a kind of pants. Wear jeans when you work outdoors.

jeans

jelly   Jelly is a food made from fruit juice and sugar. Jelly tastes good on toast or bread. **jellies.**

jet   A jet is a kind of airplane. The jet flew toward the airport. **jets.**

job   A job is the work that someone has to do. My job is to keep my room clean. His job is driving a taxi. **jobs.**

jet

joke　A **joke** is something you say or do to make people laugh. Gary told me a funny **joke.** **jokes.**

joke

judge　A **judge** decides who is right and who is wrong. Sometimes **judges** decide who wins a game. **judges.**

judge

juice　Juice is the liquid part of fruits and vegetables. Would you like some orange **juice?** **juices.**

jump　When you **jump,** you push your whole body up or off something. Jane **jumped** and caught the ball. Then she **jumped** off the side of the pool. **jumped, jumping.**

jump rope　You use a **jump rope** to play a game. You swing the rope and jump over it. **jump ropes.**

jump

jump rope

just　He is **just** walking around the block. She **just** left a minute ago.

Kk

kangaroo A kangaroo is an animal with strong back legs. A **kangaroo** can move very fast by jumping. A baby **kangaroo** is carried in a kind of pocket in front of its mother's stomach. **kangaroos.**

kangaroo

K | k

keep   Keep means to have something for a time. Can you **keep** a secret? Joy **keeps** her money in a bank. **Keep** your toys in your room. **kept, keeping.**

keep

kept   Dan **kept** his books on the shelf.

key   A **key** opens and closes a lock. Dad forgot his **key**, so he couldn't open the car door. **keys.**

key

kick   When you **kick** something, you hit it with your foot. George was **kicking** the ball. He **kicked** it into a tree. **kicked, kicking.**

kick

kid   **1.** A **kid** is a baby goat. **2. Kid** also means a child. The **kids** are riding their bikes. **kids.**

kid

kid

137

K|k

kind²

kind¹   Kind means friendly or nice. The **kind** boy helped Grandma carry the boxes. **kinder, kindest.**

kind²   Kind means a group of things that are alike in some way. Meat is a **kind** of food. Fruit and vegetables are other **kinds** of food. **kinds.**

kindergarten   Kindergarten is the year of school before first grade. **kindergartens.**

king

king   A **king** is a man who rules a country and its people. **Kings** have great power. **kings.**

kiss

kiss   Kiss means to touch with the lips. Lee's mother **kissed** him as he left. **kissed, kissing.**

kitchen   A **kitchen** is a room where food is cooked and kept. **Kitchens** have refrigerators and stoves. Many people like to eat in the **kitchen**. **kitchens.**

kitchen

K | k

kite A **kite** is a toy that you fly with a string. Most **kites** are made of light wood and paper. We like to fly kites. **kites.**

kite

kitten A **kitten** is a baby cat. **kittens.**

kitten

knee The **knee** is the part of the leg that can bend. You bend your **knees** when you walk or sit. **knees.**

knee

knew He **knew** the answer.

knife A **knife** is used to cut food and other things. **Knives** are sharp. **knives.**

knife

know Know means to have facts about someone or something. Do you **know** how to swim? Julie **knows** everyone in her class. **knew, known, knowing.**

known I have **known** Bob a long time.

L l

ladder   A **ladder** is a set of steps used to climb up and down. Dad used a **ladder** to get to the roof of our house. **ladders.**

ladder

lake A **lake** is water with land around it. You can sail a boat on a **lake**. **lakes.**

lake

lamb A **lamb** is a baby sheep. **lambs.**

lamb

lamp A **lamp** gives light. Jan turned on the **lamp** so she could read. **lamps.**

lamp

land **1.** Land is the solid part of the earth. People live on the **land,** not the water.
2. **Land** also means ground or soil. The farmer planted corn on his **land.**

language **Language** is words, spoken or written. In the United States, most people speak the English **language**. **languages.**

land

L l

lap

lap When you sit down, your upper legs become a **lap.** Sam held his little sister on his **lap. laps.**

large

large If something is **large,** it is big. The children were carrying a **large** box. **larger, largest.**

last

last¹ **Last** means coming after all others. Danny took the **last** seat in the row.

last² **Last** means to keep on. The snow **lasted** all day. How long did your bad cold **last? lasted, lasting.**

late **Late** means after the usual time. Hurry or you'll be **late** for school. **later, latest.**

laugh **Laugh** means to make happy sounds when you think something is funny. Lisa **laughed** at the clown. **laughed, laughing.**

late

leader A **leader** is someone who shows the way or goes first. Ann is the **leader** of the band. **leaders.**

leader

leaf A **leaf** is part of a tree or plant. A tree or plant has many **leaves** in summer. Most **leaves** are green. **leaves.**

leaf

learn **Learn** means to find out about something. We **learn** to read and write in school. **learned, learning.**

learn

leave 1. **Leave** means to go away. He leaves school at the same time every day. 2. **Leave** also means to go without taking something. **Leave** your books on your desk. **left, leaving.**

leaves **Leaves** change their colors in the fall.

leaves

L l

left¹

left¹ Left is the opposite direction from right. Each person has a **left** hand and a right hand. We read words from **left** to right. Turn **left** at the corner.

left² She **left** her money at home.

leg The **leg** is a part of the body. People and animals stand and move about on their **legs**. People have two **legs**. Many animals have four legs. **legs.**

leg

lemon

lemon A **lemon** is a sour, yellow fruit that grows on trees. The juice of **lemons** is used to make lemonade. **lemons.**

length Length means how long something is. The pencil is five inches in **length**. The **length** of the movie was two hours. **lengths.**

length

L l

leopard

leopard A **leopard** is a large animal like a cat. Most **leopards** have spots. **leopards.**

less Two is **less** than four. One piece of candy is **less** than two pieces of candy. There was **less** rain this year than last year.

less

lesson A **lesson** is something you learn or are taught. Molly takes piano lessons. **lessons.**

lesson

let **Let** means to not stop someone from doing something. I **let** Jane ride my bike. Will your mother **let** you go to the store? **let, letting.**

letter **1.** A **letter** is a part of the alphabet. A and B are **letters.** There are twenty-six **letters** in the alphabet. **2. Letter** also means a written note. Kathy got a **letter** from her mother. **letters.**

letter

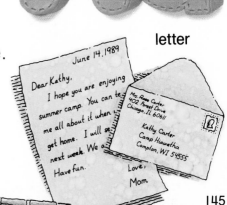

June 14, 1989

Dear Kathy,
I hope you are enjoying summer camp. You can tell me all about it when you get home. I will see you next week. We a Have fun.

Love,
Mom

Mrs. Rosa Carter
402 Forest Drive
Chicago, IL 60611

Kathy Carter
Camp Hiawatha
Compton, WI 54555

L | l

lettuce

lettuce Lettuce is a green vegetable. It is the leaves of a plant. **Lettuce** is used in salads.

librarian

librarian A librarian is someone who works in a library. You can ask the librarian for help in finding a book. **librarians.**

library

library A library is a room or building where books are kept. You can take books out at most libraries. **libraries.**

 lick

lick Lick means to move the tongue over something. Sue licked the ice cream. **licked, licking.**

life **1.** People, animals, and plants have life. Having life means being alive, breathing, and growing. Rocks do not have life.
2. Life also means the time a person, an animal, or a plant is alive. My grandfather had a long life. **lives.**

light¹

light¹   **1. Light** comes from the sun. We need **light** to see. We have **light** during the day and darkness at night. **2. Light** also means something, like a lamp or candle, that gives brightness. Turn the **light** on. **lights.**

light²   When something is **light**, it weighs very little. A rabbit is **light**, but an elephant is heavy. **lighter, lightest.**

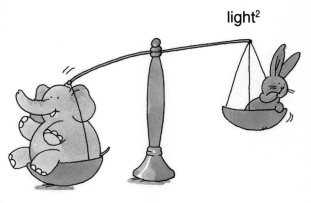

light²

lightning   **Lightning** is a flash of electricity in the sky. **Lightning** struck the tree.

lightning

like¹   **Like** means the same as. My toy is just **like** yours.

like²   **Like** means to be pleased with something or someone. Most people **like** apple pie. I **like** all my friends. **liked, liking.**

like¹

L | l

line

line   A **line** is a long, thin mark. Some **lines** are straight and some are curved. You can draw **lines** on paper. **lines.**

lion   A **lion** is a large animal like a cat. Some **lions** have long hair around their heads. **lions.**

lion

lip

lip   Your mouth has an upper **lip** and a lower **lip**. You blow through your **lips** when you whistle. **lips.**

liquid   A **liquid** is something that flows freely like water. It is not a solid or a gas. Juice and milk are **liquids**. **liquids.**

liquid

list

list   When you write your favorite toys on a piece of paper, you make a **list**. I made a **list** of things to buy at the store. **lists.**

listen   Listen means to hear or try to hear. Listen to the thunder. We listened to the band. **listened, listening.**

listen

little   If something is little, it is not big. His pet is a little kitten. **littler, littlest.**

little

live[1]   **1.** Live means to be alive, to breathe and grow. Animals live, but rocks do not.
2. Live also means to make your home in a place. We live in a big city. Squirrels live in trees. **lived, living.** Live[1] sounds like give.

live[1]

live[2]   Live means having life. We saw a real, live tiger at the fair. Live[2] sounds like drive.

lives   They say a cat has nine lives.

L l

living room   A living room is a room in a house or apartment. A living room is used by the whole family. We watch television in the living room. **living rooms.**

living room

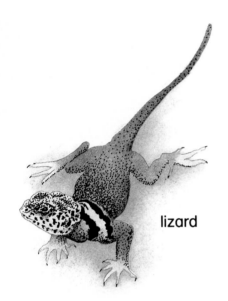
lizard

lizard   A lizard is an animal like a snake. It has four legs and a long tail. **lizards.**

lobster   A lobster is an animal that lives in the ocean. **Lobsters** have hard shells. They are good to eat. **lobsters.**

lobster

lock   A lock is used to keep something closed. Some doors and windows have **locks.** Many **locks** must be opened with keys. **locks.**

lock

150

long

long **1.** When something is **long**, it measures a lot from end to end. An inch is short, and a mile is **long**.
2. Long also means lasting for some time. We went on a **long** trip last summer. **longer, longest.**

look

look **1. Look** means to turn the eyes to see something. **Look** at that airplane!
2. Look also means to try to find. He is **looking** for his key. **looked, looking.**

lose **1.** When you **lose** something, you are not able to find it. Be careful not to **lose** your money.
2. Lose also means to not win. Did your team win or **lose**? **lost, losing.**

lost Luis **lost** his money.

lost

L l

lot

lot A **lot** means a great number or a large amount of something. There were a **lot** of birds on the roof. Ann made **lots** of sandwiches. **lots.**

loud When something is **loud**, it makes a lot of noise. The television is too loud. **louder, loudest.**

love

love 1. Love means a warm, good feeling for someone or something. Liz feels **love** for her puppy.
2. Love also means to have a warm, good feeling for someone or something. Jack **loves** all his friends. **loved, loving.**

low

low Low means near the ground, or not high. There are **low** bushes in front of our house. The wall was so **low** I climbed over it. **lower, lowest.**

lunch Lunch is a meal eaten in the middle of the day. We had sandwiches for lunch today. **lunches.**

lunch

M m

machine A **machine** has moving parts that make it work. **Machines** help people to get things done faster and more easily. Airplanes, washers, and cars are **machines. machines.**

machine

M | m

made

made   Mother **made** lemonade.

magnet   A **magnet** is a piece of metal that pulls other pieces of metal to it. Nails will stick to a **magnet**. **magnets.**

magnet

mail

mail   **1.** Letters, cards, and packages are **mail**. Mail carriers bring the mail.
2. Mail also means to send a letter, card, or package to someone. Rose **mailed** a birthday card to her aunt. **mailed, mailing.**

mailbox   A **mailbox** is a place where you mail letters or cards. A **mailbox** is also a place where mail is left for you. **mailboxes.**

mail carrier   mailbox

mail carrier   A mail carrier is a person whose job is bringing mail to people. **Mail carriers** bring letters and other mail from the post office. **mail carriers.**

make   **I.** Make means to put together or build something. Let's **make** a boat. She **made** a cake.
2. Make also means to cause something to take place. Thunder **makes** a loud noise. You **make** me laugh. **made, making.**

make

make-believe   Make-believe means not real. Dragons are make-believe animals.

make-believe

mama   Mama is another name for mother. **mamas.**

man   A boy grows up to be a **man**. Boys grow up to be **men. men.**

many   How **many** days are there in a week? There are too **many** beans on my plate. I can't eat that **many**.

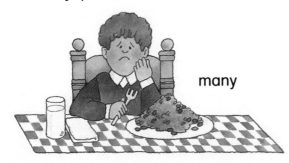

many

man

M|m

map

map   A **map** is a drawing of an area of the earth that shows many places. **Maps** show countries, cities, rivers, seas, and lakes. **maps.**

marble

marble   A **marble** is a small glass ball used to play games. **Marbles** are usually colored. **marbles.**

mark   A **mark** is a line or dot made on something. Tom made a **mark** on the wall. A period is a **mark** put at the end of a sentence. **marks.**

market   A **market** is a place where people buy and sell things. The farmer took his pigs to the **market**. **markets.**

market

match¹   A **match** is a short stick of wood or paper. The top catches fire when you rub it against some things. **Matches** can be dangerous. **matches.**

match¹

match²   **Match** means to go well together. Her sweater **matches** her socks. Choose the word in the list that **matches** each picture. **matched, matching.**

match²

math   **Math** is a short word for mathematics.

mathematics   **Mathematics** is the study of numbers. Adding and subtracting are a part of **mathematics.**

mathematics

may   **May** we go outside to play? We **may** go to the circus tonight.

maybe   **Maybe** Jan and I will go to the game. **Maybe** our team will win.

me   He saw **me** at the swimming pool. The secret is between you and **me.**

meadow   A **meadow** is a piece of land where grass grows. **meadows.**

meadow

M | m

meal A **meal** is the food eaten at one time. We eat three **meals** a day. The morning **meal** is breakfast. **meals.**

meal

mean¹ **1.** If you **mean** to do something, you plan to do it. He didn't **mean** to break the window.
2. When you know what something says, you know what it **means.** Cold **means** not hot. What does this word **mean**? **meant, meaning.**

mean²

mean² Someone who is **mean** is not nice or kind. It is **mean** to hurt someone's feelings. Cinderella's family was **mean** to her. **meaner, meanest.**

meant What do you think she **meant**? He never **meant** to hurt the cat.

measure Measure means to find the amount or size of something. The doctor **measured** Jan to see how tall she was. **measured, measuring.**

measure

meat　Meat is a kind of food that comes from animals. Hamburger and ham are kinds of **meat**.

meat

mechanic　A **mechanic** is a person whose job is fixing machines. Some **mechanics** work in garages. **mechanics.**

mechanic

medicine　Medicine is something used to make a sick person well. Doctors tell sick people what **medicine** to take. Remember to take the **medicine** for your cold. **medicines.**

medicine

meet　Meet means to come together. Would you like to **meet** Mister Rogers? **Meet** me in front of the playground. **met, meeting.**

men　Boys grow up to be **men**.

met　We **met** our friends at the park.

meet

M | m

mice Mice means more than one mouse. We saw field **mice** in the yard.

mice

microscope A microscope is used to make things look bigger. A microscope helps you see things that are too small to see with your eyes. **microscopes.**

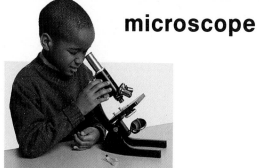

microscope

microwave A microwave is a special kind of oven. Microwaves cook food very quickly. **microwaves.**

microwave

middle The middle of something is its center. The soccer ball is in the middle of the field.

middle

might We might go ice skating if it stays cold.

milk   Milk is a drink that comes from cows. It is white. Drinking **milk** every day helps you grow.

milk

mind   The **mind** is the part of a person that thinks and feels. You use your **mind** to learn and to imagine. **minds.**

mine   That bike is **mine.**

mine

minute   A **minute** is a short period of time. Sixty seconds equal one **minute.** Sixty **minutes** equal one hour. **minutes.**

minute

miss   **1.** To **miss** something means not to get it. Lucy tried to catch the ball, but **missed** it. She **missed** her bus. **2. Miss** also means to feel bad because someone is gone. Maria **missed** her family when she was away at camp. **missed, missing.**

miss

M | m

mitten

Miss   Miss is used before the name of a woman who is not married. A young girl is sometimes called Miss. **Misses.**

mitten   A mitten covers the hand. It has a special place for the thumb. Mittens keep your hands warm when it is cold outside. **mittens.**

mix

mom

mix   Mix means to put together. You mix eggs, sugar, chocolate, and other things to make these cookies. **mixed, mixing.**

mom   Mom is another name for mother. **moms.**

money   Pennies, nickels, dimes, and dollars are money. People buy things with money. People who work at jobs are paid money.

money

M | m

monkey　A **monkey** is an animal with long arms and legs. There are many different kinds of **monkeys**. Some **monkeys** live in trees. **monkeys.**

monkey

monster　A **monster** is a make-believe person or animal. **Monsters** are big or scary. In stories, some **monsters** are friendly and some are not. Dragons are **monsters. monsters.**

monster

month　A **month** is a part of a year. There are twelve **months** in a year. They are January, February, March, April, May, June, July, August, September, October, November, and December. **months.**

moon

moon　The **moon** is the biggest and brightest thing in the sky at night. The **moon** goes around the earth.

M | m

mop

mop   You use a **mop** to clean the floor. A **mop** has a long handle. **mops.**

more   A dime is **more** than a penny. I would like **more** soup. This picture is **more** beautiful than that one.

morning   Morning is the early part of the day. **Morning** ends at noon. **mornings.**

morning

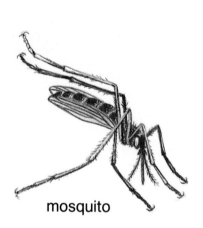
mosquito

mosquito   A **mosquito** is an insect that flies. Some **mosquitoes** bite people. **mosquitoes.**

most   Sam did the **most** work. **Most** people like pizza. The **most** beautiful kitten is the black one.

mother   A **mother** is a woman who has a child or children. **Mothers** and fathers are parents. **mothers.**

mother

motor A **motor** is a kind of machine that makes other machines work. **Motors** run on electricity or gas. Cars have **motors** that make them move. **motors.**

motor

mountain A **mountain** is a very high hill. Some **mountains** have snow on top. **mountains.**

mountain

mouse A **mouse** is a small animal with a long tail. Some **mice** live in people's houses. Some **mice** live in fields and meadows. **mice.**

mouse

mouth The **mouth** is the part of the body that helps you eat and talk. It is part of the face. Your teeth and tongue are in your **mouth. mouths.**

mouth

M | m

move

move   Move means to go from one place to another. May I **move** to a different desk? Her family **moved** to a new house. **moved, moving.**

movie   A **movie** tells a story with pictures. Bob loves to watch **movies.** **movies.**

movie

Mr.	Mrs. or Ms.	Ms. or Miss

Mr.   Mr. is used before a man's name.

Mrs.   Mrs. is used before a married woman's name.

Ms.   Ms. is used before a woman's name.

much   How **much** time do we have for swimming? I like swimming very **much.**

muscle   A **muscle** is a part of the body that helps you move. Without **muscles**, you could not lift or carry things. There are over 600 **muscles** in your body. **muscles.**

muscle

music   The sounds made by a piano, a violin, a guitar, and other instruments are **music**. The sound of a person singing is **music**. People like to listen to **music**.

music

must   I would like to stay, but I **must** leave. I **must** go home for dinner now.

my   I lost **my** mittens in the park. I was playing with **my** friends.

myself   I saw **myself** in the mirror.

myself

167

Nn

nail   **1.** A nail is a thin piece of metal with a point at one end. **Nails** hold pieces of wood together.
2. Nail also means the hard part at the end of a finger or toe. **nails.**

nail

name Your **name** is what people call you. Everyone has a **name**. Countries and cities also have **names**. The players' **names** are on their shirts. **names.**

name

nap A **nap** is a short sleep. Do you take an afternoon nap? **naps.**

nap

napkin A **napkin** is a piece of cloth or paper. **Napkins** are used at meals to protect clothes and to clean the lips and fingers. **napkins.**

napkin

nature **Nature** means everything not made by people. Plants, animals, air, water, and people are part of **nature**. The earth and its mountains, oceans, and rivers are part of **nature**.

N | n

neck

near Her birthday is **near**. We are **near** the toy store. **nearer, nearest.**

neck The **neck** is the part of the body between the head and shoulders. **necks.**

necklace

need

necklace A **necklace** is something worn around the neck. Mom wore a beautiful **necklace** at the party. **necklaces.**

need When you **need** something, you must have it. The hungry people **need** food. Plants **need** water. Tom **needs** new gloves this winter. **needed, needing.**

neighbor A **neighbor** is a person who lives close to you. Our **neighbors** are working in their yard. **neighbors.**

neighbor

neighborhood   A **neighborhood** is the part of town where you live. There is a small park in our **neighborhood**. **neighborhoods.**

neighborhood

nest   A **nest** is a kind of home birds build. It is shaped like a bowl. **Nests** are made from straw, leaves, and other things. Baby birds live in **nests**. **nests.**

nest

net   A **net** is made of string. The string is tied together to make a kind of cloth with holes. There is a **net** on the ring you throw a basketball through. **Nets** are also used to catch fish. **nets.**

net

never   I have **never** met a monster. I hope I **never** will.

new   New means not old, or not used yet. We have **new** kittens at home. Her bike is new. **newer, newest.**

new

171

N | n

newspaper

A **newspaper** is sheets of paper printed with stories that tell what is happening. Many people read **newspapers** every day. **newspapers.**

newspaper

next

We will catch the **next** bus. Sit **next** to me.

next

nice

Nice means good or kind. I had a **nice** time. It was **nice** of you to help me. **nicer, nicest.**

nickel

nickel

A **nickel** is a kind of money. One **nickel** equals five cents. **nickels.**

night

Night is the time between evening and morning. We sleep at **night**. Nights are dark. **nights.**

night

no   There are **no** oranges left.
Just say **no** if you don't
want to play.

no

noise   **Noise** means a sound we
do not want to hear. The
loud **noise** woke me up.
noises.

noise

none   **None** of the children smiled. We
wanted a cake, but the bakery had
none left.

noon   **Noon** is 12 o'clock in the daytime.
Noon is the middle of the day. We
eat lunch at **noon.**

noon

N | n

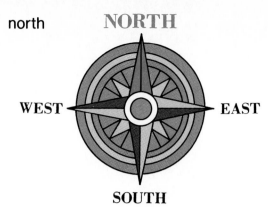

north

NORTH

WEST **EAST**

SOUTH

north   North is the direction opposite to south. If you look at the sun when it comes up, **north** is on your left.

nose

nose   Your **nose** is in the middle of your face. **Noses** help us smell things. **noses.**

not   I am **not** surprised. It's **not** time to leave. Tom is **not** at home.

note   A **note** is a very short letter. My aunt sent me a **note** on my birthday. **notes.**

note

nothing   He saw **nothing** he wanted to buy.

now   Do the job **now**. We are leaving **now**.

number   A number is a word that tells how many. 2, 9, and 15 are **numbers**. You use numbers in math. **numbers.**

number

nurse   A nurse is a person whose job is taking care of sick people. Some **nurses** work in hospitals. Some **nurses** visit homes. **nurses.**

nurse

nut   A nut is a seed or a dry fruit. **Nuts** have hard shells. Most **nuts** grow on trees. Some **nuts** are good to eat. **nuts.**

nut

Oo

oak An **oak** is a kind of tree. We sat under the **oak** to get out of the sun. **oaks.**

oak

object An object is something you can see or touch. A chair, a book, and a pencil are objects. How many objects can you carry in your pocket? **objects.**

object

observe When we observe something, we look at it carefully and learn about it. We learn things from looking, listening, smelling, tasting, and touching. We use all our senses to help us observe. **observed, observing.**

observe

ocean An ocean is salt water that covers much of the earth. Fish and whales are some animals that live in the ocean. Sea is another word for ocean. **oceans.**

ocean

o'clock O'clock is a word we use to say what time it is. I eat my lunch at 12 o'clock.

octopus An octopus is an animal that lives in the sea. It has a soft body and eight arms. **octopuses.**

octopus

O|o

off

of   This book **of** mine is all about monsters. My toy dinosaur is made **of** plastic.

off   I took **off** my coat. Jill pushed me **off** the swing. Mark's birthday is only three days **off.**

office   An **office** is a place where people work. My mother took me to visit her **office. offices.**

office

often   If something happens **often**, it happens many times. When we watch a movie, we **often** eat popcorn.

oil

oil   **Oil** is a thick liquid. Some **oil** comes from under the ground. **Oil** helps machines to work. We cook with **oil** that comes from animals and plants.

O|o

old Someone who is **old** has lived for a long time. My grandmother is **old** and I am young. **older, oldest.**

old

on The paper is **on** the desk. The TV is **on.** I talked to Bill **on** the phone. I put my hat **on.**

on

once If something happens one time, it happens **once.** Jan has a piano lesson **once** a week.

onion An **onion** is a vegetable with a strong smell. The part we eat grows under the ground. **onions.**

onion

only Our dog is the **only** pet we have. Sue is the **only** girl on the baseball team.

only

179

O|o

open

open

When you **open** something, people and things can get in or out of it. We **opened** the car window, and a butterfly flew in. That store **opens** at 9 o'clock. **opened, opening.**

opposite

opposite

When two things are as different from each other as they can be, they are **opposites**. Short is the **opposite** of tall. **opposites.**

or

I can play outside with my football **or** inside with my pet turtle. Hurry up **or** you will be late.

orange

orange

I. An **orange** is a fruit that grows on a tree. **Oranges** are used to make **orange** juice. **oranges.**
2. **Orange** also is a color. Oranges and pumpkins are **orange**.

order

Order is the way one thing comes after another in a special way. The children lined up in **order** of size. The words in the dictionary are in alphabetical **order**.

order

other　The **other** children got dirty at the playground, but we did not. We'll go to the zoo some **other** day.

other

our　**Our** garden looked beautiful, but their garden did not.

our

out　The bird was not in its cage because it flew **out.** The firefighter put **out** the fire. Tom did not go **out** to play because he was sick.

outside　Mom and Sue waited **outside** for the mail carrier to come. The **outside** of the carrot was dirty so we had to wash it.

outside

O|o

oven

oven   An **oven** is the part of a stove that you use to bake things. The bread is ready to come out of the **oven**. **ovens.**

over   Can you come **over** to my house after school? The robin flew **over** the trees. The milk ran **over** the edge of the glass.

over

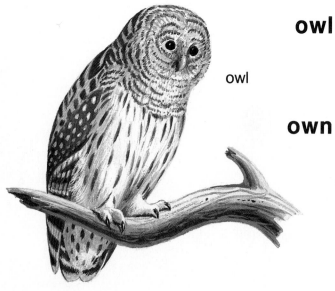

owl

owl   An **owl** is a bird with a big head and big eyes. **Owls** fly around at night. **owls.**

own   **1.** When you **own** something, it is yours to keep. Do you **own** a bicycle? I **own** lots of books. **owned, owning.**
2. Something that is your **own** belongs to you. I want to have a room of my **own**.

Pp

pad A **pad** is a large, floating leaf. The frog sat on the lily **pad. pads.**

pad

P | p

page

page A **page** is one side of a sheet of paper. Turn the **page.** Books have many **pages. pages.**

pail

pail A **pail** is used to hold something in. Use a shovel to fill your **pail** with sand. **pails.**

paint

paint **I.** Paint is a liquid used to color things. **Paint** comes in many different colors. Dad chose blue **paint** for my room. **paints.**
2. Paint also means to cover something with this liquid. Mom **painted** the kitchen yellow. **painted, painting.**

painter

painter A **painter** is a person who paints. Some **painters** paint houses. Some **painters** paint pictures. **painters.**

pair

pair A **pair** is two things that go together. He lost a **pair** of mittens. **pairs.**

pajamas   Pajamas are clothes to sleep in. Pajamas have a shirt and pants. Sally bought yellow **pajamas.**

pajamas

pan   A pan is something to cook food in. Use this pan to fry the eggs. **pans.**

pancake   A pancake is a small, flat cake that is fried. Let's make pancakes for breakfast. **pancakes.**

pancake

panda   A panda is a large animal. Pandas are black and white and look like bears. There are very few pandas alive today. **pandas.**

panda

pants   Pants are clothes you wear on the lower part of your body. Some pants are long. Some pants are short.

pants

P | p

paper

papa   Papa is a name for father. **papas.**

paper   Paper is used to write on and to make bags. It is made from wood. The pages of books are made of paper.

parade

parade   A parade is a group of people walking together in rows down a street. Some **parades** also have people in cars. There were clowns and animals in the circus **parade. parades.**

parakeet

parakeet   A parakeet is a bird with brightly colored feathers. It has a very long tail. **Parakeets** are often kept as pets. **parakeets.**

parent   A parent is a mother or father. Paul's **parents** came to school. **parents.**

park **1.** A park is an area of land with grass and trees. People can use **parks** for walking and playing. Some **parks** have playgrounds. **parks.**
2. Park also means to leave a car someplace for a time. Mother **parked** the car in the garage. **parked, parking.**

park

part

part A part is a piece of something, but not the whole thing. All of these **parts** fit together to make a model car. John ate only **part** of his lunch. **parts.**

party A party is a group of people having a good time. Alex went to the birthday **party. parties.**

party

pass **1.** Pass means to go by. I **pass** the store on my way to school.
2. Pass also means to hand something from one person to another. Please **pass** the butter. **passed, passing.**

pass

P | p

paste

past
1. Past means gone by or ended. Summer is **past**. This **past** weekend we went to the circus.
2. When you go **past** something, you go by it or beyond it. The children ran **past** our house.

paste
Paste is used to make things stick together. Charles used **paste** to stick the pieces of paper together.

path

path
A **path** is made when people or animals travel over the same ground a lot. **Paths** are not wide enough for cars. We like to walk on the **path** through the woods. **paths.**

paw

paw
A **paw** is the foot of an animal that has nails. Cats and dogs have paws. **paws.**

pea

pea
A **pea** is a small, round vegetable. Peas are green and grow on vines. **peas.**

peach

P|p

peach A **peach** is a round fruit that grows on trees. **Peaches** are juicy and have a fuzzy skin. **peaches.**

peanut A **peanut** is a kind of seed that looks like a nut. **Peanuts** grow in shells under the ground. They are used to make **peanut** butter. **peanuts.**

peanut

peanut butter Peanut butter is a food made from peanuts. **Peanut butter** is soft and is eaten in sandwiches.

peanut butter

pear A **pear** is a sweet, juicy fruit. **Pears** are green or yellow, and grow on trees. **pears.**

pear

peek Peek means to look quickly at something. Steve **peeked** at the presents in the closet. **peeked, peeking.**

P p

pen   A **pen** is used for writing. **Pens** are often made of plastic. There is ink in a **pen**. **pens.**

pencil   A **pencil** is used for writing and drawing. A **pencil** must have a sharp point to write well. **pencils.**

pen

pencil

penny   A **penny** is a kind of money. It is another word for a cent. There are one hundred **pennies** in a dollar. **pennies.**

penny

people   Men, women, and children are **people.** There were many **people** at the picnic.

people

period   **1.** A **period** is one of the lengths of time in a school day. We will have a story in the next **period.**
2. A **period** is a dot at the end of a sentence. **periods.**

period

READING IS FUN.

person   A **person** is any boy, girl, man, or woman. **persons.**

pet   A **pet** is a favorite animal that you take care of. Liz has both a cat and a dog as **pets**. **pets.**

pet

phone   You use a **phone** to talk to someone who is in another place. A **phone** is another word for a telephone. **phones.**

phone

piano   A **piano** makes music. You play the **piano** with your fingers. **pianos.**

pick   1. **Pick** means to choose. He **picked** the red wagon.
2. **Pick** also means to pull with the fingers. I **picked** some flowers in the garden. **picked, picking.**

piano

picnic   A **picnic** is a party with a meal outdoors. People have **picnics** in the summer. **picnics.**

picture   A **picture** is something that you draw or paint. Jack drew a **picture** of his house. **pictures.**

picture

P p

pie

piece

pie   Pie is a kind of food. **Pies** are baked in an oven. Would you like some apple pie? **pies.**

piece   A piece is one of the parts into which something is divided. A puzzle may have many **pieces**. Kim cut the pie into **pieces**. **pieces.**

pillow

pilot

pig

pig   A pig is an animal with a fat body, short legs, and a curly tail. **pigs.**

pillow   A pillow is something soft you rest your head on when you sleep. **pillows.**

pilot   A pilot is a person who flies an airplane or helicopter. **pilots.**

pin   A pin is used to hold things together. It has one sharp end to stick through things. **pins.**

pink   Pink is a color. It is made by mixing red and white. Your tongue is **pink**. Some roses are **pink**.

pink

pizza   Pizza is a kind of food. It is made of round, flat bread covered with cheese, tomatoes, and other things. **Pizzas** are baked in an oven. **pizzas.**

pizza

place   A **place** is where a person or thing is. Our town is a nice **place** to live. Here is a **place** to sit. **places.**

plan   Plan means to think about how something will be done. Bob **planned** a party for his sister. **planned, planning.**

plane   A **plane** is a machine that can fly. **Planes** have wings and engines. Another word for **plane** is airplane. **planes.**

plane

P | p

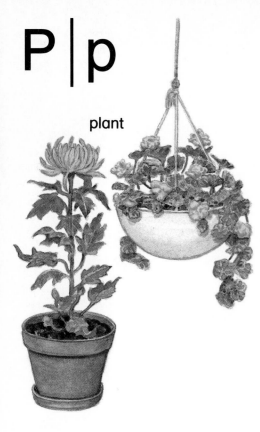

plant

plant A **plant** is a living thing. A **plant** can make its own food from sunlight, air, and water. **Plants** cannot move about. Trees, bushes, flowers, and grass are **plants. plants.**

plastic Plastic is used to make many things. It can be shaped when it is hot. It becomes hard when it is cool. **Plastic** can be very strong. It can be hard or soft.

plastic

plate

plate A plate is a flat dish. We eat food from plates. **plates.**

play

play **I.** Play means to have fun. Let's play after school. **played, playing. 2.** Play also means a story that is acted. Carol is in her class play. **plays.**

playground A playground is a place to play outside. Some **playgrounds** have swings. **playgrounds.**

please   Please pass the milk. Would you please be quiet? He is easy to please. **pleased, pleasing.**

plenty

plenty   Plenty means enough. There is plenty of food for everyone.

pocket   A pocket is a small bag sewed into your clothes for carrying things. Lee's jacket has four pockets. **pockets.**

pocket

poem   A poem uses rhyme
To say something well,
To share a good thought,
Or a story to tell.
poems.

point   1. A point means a sharp end. The pencil has a sharp point. **points.**
2. Point also means to show something with your finger. Mom pointed to the rabbit in our yard. **pointed, pointing.**

point

P p

poke

poke   Poke means to push. Jean poked me with her finger. **poked, poking.**

polar bear   A polar bear is a large, white bear. Polar bears live in cold places. **polar bears.**

polar bear

pole   A pole is a long piece of wood or metal. We need a pole to get the ball out of the tree. **poles.**

pond   A pond is water with land all around it. A pond is smaller than a lake. **ponds.**

pond

pony   A pony is a small horse. People like to ride ponies. **ponies.**

pony

pool   A pool is a place to swim. Some pools are inside buildings. Some pools are outside. **pools.**

pool

Pp

popcorn

Popcorn is a kind of corn that opens and makes a noise when you heat it. **Popcorn** is fun to make.

popcorn

porcupine

A porcupine is a small animal. Its back, sides, and tail are covered with sharp points called quills. **porcupines.**

porcupine

poster

A poster is a large printed piece of paper put up for everyone to see. Look at the circus **poster**. **posters.**

poster

post office

You can mail a letter at the post office. Mail carriers bring mail to you from the post office. **post offices.**

pot

pot

A pot is used to hold things. Some pots are for cooking. Some **pots** hold plants or flowers. Dad made a big **pot** of soup. **pots.**

potato

A potato is a vegetable. The part we eat grows under the ground. **potatoes.**

potato

P | p

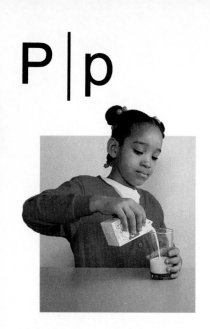

pour

pour   When you **pour** a liquid, it flows from one place to another. Cathy **poured** a glass of milk. **poured, pouring.**

practice   Practice means to do something again and again. People **practice** in order to get better at doing things. Bill **practices** the piano every day. **practiced, practicing.**

present

present   A **present** is something you give someone or someone gives you. Ann got a birthday **present** from her friend. **presents.**

pretend

pretend   Pretend means to make believe that something is real when it is not. Let's **pretend** to be astronauts. **pretended, pretending.**

pretty

pretty   Pretty means that something we see or hear is nice. Those flowers are **pretty**. I think the red flowers are **prettier** than the blue. **prettier, prettiest.**

198

prince | A **prince** is the son of a king or a queen. There are many stories about princes. **princes.**

prince

princess

princess | A **princess** is the daughter of a king or a queen. There are many stories about princesses. **princesses.**

print | Print means to write so that the letters do not touch each other. Jim **printed** his name at the top of the page. **printed, printing.**

print

prize | A **prize** is something you win for doing something well. Chris won a **prize** in the race. **prizes.**

prize

problem | A **problem** is something that needs to be worked out. What is the answer to this math **problem**? Making friends in a new town can be a problem. **problems.**

P | p

protect

project   A **project** is a plan for doing something. Grace and her friends have a big **project**—they are building a tree house. **projects.**

protect   **Protect** means to keep someone or something safe. **Protect** your eyes when you work with tools. **protected, protecting.**

proud   **Proud** means thinking well of yourself or others. Ruth was **proud** of her team. **prouder, proudest.**

pull

pull   **Pull** means to move something toward you. It is hard to **pull** weeds from the ground. The dogs **pulled** the sled a long way. **pulled, pulling.**

pumpkin

pumpkin   A **pumpkin** is a large orange fruit. **Pumpkins** grow on vines. They are used for making pies. **pumpkins.**

puppet   A puppet is a toy that looks like a person or an animal. You put some **puppets** over your hand and move them with your fingers. Other **puppets** are moved by strings from above. **puppets.**

puppet

puppy   A puppy is a baby dog. **puppies.**

puppy

purple   Purple is a color. It is made by mixing red and blue. Some grapes are **purple**.

purple

push   Push means to move something away from you. Dad **pushed** the door open. **pushed, pushing.**

push

put   Put means to place or set something somewhere. She **put** her book on the table. **put, putting.**

puzzle   A puzzle is a kind of game. Some **puzzles** have many pieces. Some **puzzles** are worked out with pencil and paper. **puzzles.**

puzzle

Q q

quarter

quarter   A quarter is a kind of money. It is equal to 25 cents. Four **quarters** make one dollar. **quarters.**

queen   A queen is a woman who rules a country. **Queens** have great power. **queens.**

queen

question A question is a sentence that asks something you want to know. When you ask a question, you want an answer. **questions.**

Is Jim home?

question

quick When something is quick, it has great speed. The trip across the ocean by jet was quick. Kay gave a quick answer to the teacher's question. **quicker, quickest.**

quiet Quiet means not noisy. Peter was quiet when he came home. A quiet room is best for studying. **quieter, quietest.**

quiet

quilt

quilt A quilt is a soft cover for a bed. Sue's quilt keeps her warm at night. **quilts.**

Rr

rabbit   A **rabbit** is a small animal with long ears. **Rabbits** have long back legs and can hop very fast. **rabbits.**

rabbit

raccoon   A **raccoon** is a small animal with thick fur. Its tail is long, and has rings of a lighter color. **Raccoons** look for food at night. **raccoons.**

raccoon

race   **Race** means to run very fast. We **raced** to the corner. **raced, racing.**

radio   A **radio** is something you can turn on and listen to. You can hear the voices of people far away by listening to the **radio. radios.**

radio

rain   **1.** The drops of water that fall from clouds are called **rain.** We shared an umbrella in the **rain.**
2. Rain also means to fall as drops of water. It has started to **rain. rained, raining.**

rain

rainbow   A **rainbow** is a curved band of many colors. It stretches across the sky. When the rain stopped, we saw a **rainbow** in the sky. **rainbows.**

rainbow

R | r

raincoat

raincoat — A raincoat helps you stay dry when it rains. **raincoats.**

raise

raise — **1.** When you **raise** something, you move it up. Jill **raises** her hand when she wants to speak in school.
2. Raise also means to take care of something and help it grow. The farmer **raised** corn and chickens. **raised, raising.**

raisin

raisin — A raisin is a small, sweet fruit. Raisins are dried grapes. **raisins.**

rake

rake — A rake is a kind of tool. Rakes are used in yards or gardens. **rakes.**

ran — Jill ran all the way home.

rang — When the morning bell rang, we went in to school.

raspberry — A raspberry is a small red or black fruit. Raspberries grow on bushes. **raspberries.**

raspberry

rat

rat   A **rat** is an animal that looks like a large mouse. **Rats** have long, thin tails. **rats.**

reach   **1.** When you **reach**, you hold out your arm and hand. Jim **reached** for the apple.
2. Reach also means to get to some person or place. The letter **reached** me last week. The river flows many miles to **reach** the sea. **reached, reaching.**

reach

read¹   **Read** means to look at and understand written words. Max is **reading** a story. **read, reading.**
Read¹ sounds like need.

read¹

read²   Max **read** a story to Ellen yesterday. Read² sounds like bed.

ready   To be **ready** means to be all set to do something. Lee is **ready** for the party.

ready

R | r

real Something that is **real** is true, not make-believe. Pandas are **real**, but unicorns are not **real**.

real

really Really means truly. Is Dan **really** moving away? I **really** don't know.

reason A **reason** explains why something happened. What is your **reason** for not coming to the party? **reasons.**

record A **record** is something we can put on a special machine to play music. **Records** are round and flat. They are made of plastic. **records.**

record

rectangle

rectangle A **rectangle** is a shape with four square corners. **rectangles.**

red

red Red is a color. Strawberries are **red**. Milly's wagon is bright **red**.

refrigerator A refrigerator is used to keep food cold. **Refrigerators** are kept in the kitchen. **refrigerators.**

refrigerator

remember When you **remember** something, you keep it in your mind. Did you **remember** to bring your lunch? **remembered, remembering.**

report A **report** tells the facts about something. Kim's **report** was on Alaska. She gave her **report** to the class. **reports.**

rest

rest **1.** When you **rest**, you stay quiet. After playing hard, Meg **rested**. **rested, resting.**
2. **Rest** also means the part that is left. Would you like the **rest** of this fruit?

restaurant A **restaurant** is a place where you can buy a meal. **Restaurants** have many kinds of food to choose from. **restaurants.**

restaurant

R | r

return

return   Return means to bring back or to come back. Cal **returned** his library books, and then **returned** home. **returned, returning.**

review   When you **review** something, you look at it again. Please **review** your spelling list. **reviewed, reviewing.**

revise

revise   When you **revise** something, you change it. Ben **revised** his report by correcting all the mistakes. **revised, revising.**

rhinoceros

rhinoceros   A rhinoceros is a very large animal. It has thick skin and either one or two horns. **Rhinoceroses** eat grass and other plants. **rhinoceroses.**

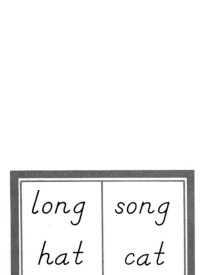

long	song
hat	cat
big	pig
go	sl_w

rhyme

rhyme   Words that end with the same sound **rhyme**. "Long" and "song" **rhyme**. What **rhymes** with "go"? **rhymed, rhyming.**

rice

rich

rich

R | r

rice Rice is a kind of food. It is often white, but can also be brown. **Rice** grows on a kind of grass.

rich **1.** **Rich** means having a very large amount of money. We read a story about a **rich** family.
2. Food that has a lot of butter and eggs is **rich**. The cake was so **rich** Jim could only eat a small piece. **richer, richest.**

ridden Lynn had **ridden** her bicycle all morning.

riddle A **riddle** is a puzzle that asks a question. **Riddles** are often funny. Here is a **riddle**: "Six people are under one small umbrella. Why don't they get wet?" "It isn't raining!" **riddles.**

riddle

R | r

ride

ride When you **ride** something, it carries you along. Jill is **riding** her bike. Tom **rode** a horse. **rode, ridden, riding.**

right

right 1. When something is **right**, it is the way it should be. **Right** is the opposite of wrong. Tim had the **right** answer to the riddle.
2. **Right** also means the opposite of left. Stacey draws with her **right** hand.

ring¹ A **ring** is round and is worn on the finger. Beth wore her new **ring**. **rings.**

ring¹   ring²

ring² **Ring** means to make a sound like that of a bell. I heard the telephone ring. **rang, rung, ringing.**

river

river A **river** is a long stream of running water. It flows into a lake or ocean. A **river** has land on both sides of it. **Rivers** are bigger than streams. **rivers.**

road A road is a way to go between places. Cars and trucks are driven on roads. **roads.**

road

robin A robin is a bird. The front part of a robin is red. Robins are found in most places in the United States. **robins.**

robin

robot A robot is a machine that is run by a computer. Robots help people to do work. Robots can look like people. **robots.**

robot

rock Rock is very hard and is found in the ground. Mountains are made of rock. He threw a rock into the lake. **rocks.**

rode Jill rode her new bike. Tom rode a horse.

roll Roll means to move by turning over and over. Kate's ball rolled down the hill. **rolled, rolling.**

roll

213

R | r

roller skate

A roller skate is a shoe, or something you wear on a shoe, that has four wheels. **Roller skates** are used to skate on a floor, a sidewalk, or something else that is smooth. **roller skates.**

roller skate

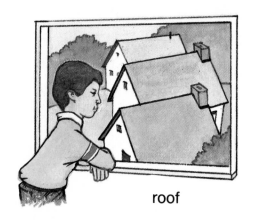

roof

roof

The top covering of a building is the **roof.** Ken can see many **roofs** from his apartment. **roofs.**

room

A **room** is part of the inside of a building. Each **room** has walls of its own. There are living **rooms,** dining **rooms,** and other kinds of **rooms.** **rooms.**

rooster

A rooster is a kind of full-grown chicken. **Roosters** crow when the sun comes up each morning. **roosters.**

rooster

R | r

root   The part of a plant that grows below the ground is the **root**. Plants get food and water through their roots. **roots.**

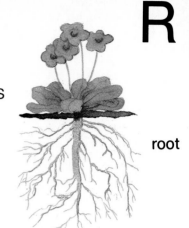
root

rope   **Rope** is made of very thick string twisted together. **Rope** is used to tie things. **ropes.**

rose   A **rose** is a kind of flower. **Roses** smell sweet and are often red, pink, or yellow. **roses.**

rose

round   When something is **round**, it is shaped like a circle. Wheels are round. **rounder, roundest.**

row

row   When things are in a **row**, they are in a straight line. The cars are parked in a **row**. **rows.**

rug   A **rug** is something that covers the floor. **Rugs** can be large or small. **rugs.**

rug

R | r

rule

rule **1.** A **rule** tells us what we must or must not do. It is a **rule** in our house that we put away our toys. **rules.**
2. Rule also means to have a lot of power over a country and its people. Many years ago a bad king **ruled** the land. **ruled, ruling.**

ruler A **ruler** is used to measure how long something is. **Rulers** also help to draw straight lines. **rulers.**

ruler

run When you **run**, you move your legs very fast. Jack **ran** after his dog. He has **run** after his dog many times. **ran, run, running.**

run

rung The bell has **rung**.

rush When you **rush**, you move in a hurry. Ken **rushed** out the door. **rushed, rushing.**

Ss

sad When you are **sad**, you feel bad about things. Jay was **sad** when his friend moved. **sadder, saddest.**

sad

S | s

safe

safe Safe means to be in no danger of harm. During the storm, Ben was **safe** at home. **safer, safest.**

safety Safety means freedom from harm. Rules about **safety** are important.

said She **said** she would help us.

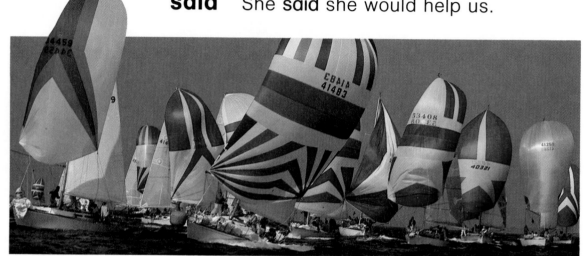

sail

sail **1.** A **sail** is a large piece of cloth used on some boats. **Sails** catch wind and help boats move. **sails.** **2.** Sail also means to move across water in a boat. We **sailed** across the lake. **sailed, sailing.**

salt

salt White grains of **salt** are added to food to make it taste better. **Salt** comes from the sea or the earth.

salty When something is **salty**, it has a lot of salt in it. Tears are **salty**. This ham tastes **salty**. **saltier, saltiest.**

same   When things are the **same**, they are alike. You and I have the **same** name.

same

sand   **Sand** is made of tiny bits of broken rock. This beach is made of **sand**.

sand

sandwich   A **sandwich** is a kind of food. It is made of two pieces of bread with meat, peanut butter, or other food in between. **sandwiches.**

sandwich

sang   Mother **sang** a song to the baby.

sank

sank   The boat hit the rock and **sank**.

sat   Dad **sat** in his favorite chair.

sat

S | s

save

1. Save means to keep someone from harm. Nick **saved** his friend from being hurt.
2. When you **save** something, you keep it for later use. David is **saving** money for a bike. **saved, saving.**

save

saw¹ A saw is a tool used to cut wood. It has sharp metal teeth. **saws.**

saw¹

saw² Ann **saw** a beautiful red bird today.

say When you **say** something, you are speaking out loud. Did Tom **say** he would be late? **said, saying.**

scare

scare Scare means to make someone feel that something bad might happen. Storms **scare** me. **scared, scaring.**

school School is a place where you learn things. We learn to read in **school**. **schools.**

school

science Science tells us why things are the way they are. We learn about the earth, the sky, animals, and people when we study **science**.

scientist A scientist is a person who tries to find out why things are the way they are. **scientists.**

scientist

scissors Scissors are used to cut things. A pair of **scissors** has two sharp edges that work together to cut paper or cloth.

scissors

sea The sea is salt water that covers much of the earth. Ocean is another word for **sea. seas.**

sea

seal A seal is an animal that lives in the sea. Seals have thick fur. **seals.**

seal

S|s

season

season   A **season** is one of the four parts of the year. The **seasons** are spring, summer, fall, and winter. **seasons.**

second[1]   When something is **second**, it is the next after the first. B is the **second** letter of the alphabet.

second[1]

second[2]

second[2]   A **second** is a very short period of time. Sixty **seconds** equal one minute. **seconds.**

secret   A **secret** is something you promise not to tell. The surprise party for Mom is a **secret**. **secrets.**

secret

see   When you **see** something, you look at it with your eyes. Did you **see** the red bird? **saw, seen, seeing.**

seed A **seed** is the part of a plant that grows into a new plant. If you put bean **seeds** in the ground, they can grow into bean plants. **seeds.**

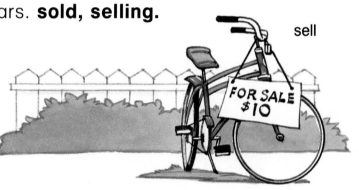

seed

seem You **seem** sad. My dog **seems** to like that bone. **seemed, seeming.**

seen Have you **seen** the beautiful bird?

sell **Sell** means to give something in return for money. Dave will **sell** his bike for ten dollars. **sold, selling.**

sell

send **Send** means to cause someone or something to go from one place to another. I **sent** her a letter. Dad **sent** me out to play. **sent, sending.**

send

sense Sight, smell, taste, hearing, and touch are the five **senses.** Dogs have a very good **sense** of smell. **senses.**

sense

S | s

sentence

sent Mom **sent** me to the store.

sentence A **sentence** is a group of words that tells a complete idea. A **sentence** begins with a capital letter. It ends with a period, a question mark, or an exclamation mark. **sentences.**

set

sew

set **1.** Set means to put something in place. **Set** the books on that table. **2.** Set also means to go down. The sun **set** at 8 o'clock. **set, setting.**

sew Sew means to push a needle and thread through cloth. Pat likes to sew. **sewed, sewing.**

shadow

shadow A **shadow** is a dark shape. It is made when something blocks the light. On sunny days, you can see your **shadow. shadows.**

shake   Shake means to move up and down quickly. **Shake** the juice before you pour it. **shook, shaken, shaking.**

shake

shaken   The medicine must be shaken before you take it.

shall   I shall go to the party.

shape   The shape of something is the way it looks. Wheels are round in shape. The cake was in the shape of a heart. **shapes.**

shape

share   When you share, you let someone use something with you. The twins share a room. **shared, sharing.**

share

sharp   Something that has a point or thin edge is sharp. This pin has a sharp point. **sharper, sharpest.**

sharp

she   Who is she? She is my teacher.

S | s

sheep

sheep   A **sheep** is an animal. Its thick, long hair is used to make cloth. Some farmers raise **sheep**. **sheep.**

sheet

sheet   **1.** A **sheet** is a large piece of cloth used on a bed. A bed usually has a top **sheet** and a bottom **sheet**.
2. A **sheet** is also a piece of paper. I took a **sheet** of paper. **sheets.**

shell

shell   A **shell** is a hard covering. Turtles and lobsters have **shells**. Eggs and nuts have **shells**. **shells.**

shine   **Shine** means to give off a bright light. The sun **shines** brightest at noon. **shone, shining.**

ship   A **ship** is a very large boat that travels on oceans or large lakes. People crossed the ocean by **ship** before there were planes. **ships.**

ship

shirt A shirt is a kind of clothing you wear over your chest and arms. Some **shirts** have buttons. **shirts.**

shirt

shoe A shoe is something you wear on your foot. Fran's **shoes** are blue, and Don's **shoes** are brown. **shoes.**

shoe

shone The sun **shone** brightly yesterday.

shook Kay **shook** the bottle.

shook

shop 1. A shop is a place where things are sold. There are two **shops** on our street. **shops.**
2. Shop also means to go to stores to buy things. I like to **shop** at the grocery. **shopped, shopping.**

shop

S|s

short

short

I. When something is **short**, it does not reach far from end to end. I live a **short** distance from school. Jill is **short** and her friend Lou is tall.
2. **Short** also means not lasting long. We played for a **short** time after lunch. **shorter, shortest.**

shot

shot

When you are given a **shot**, medicine goes under your skin through a needle. People get **shots** so they won't get sick. **shots.**

should

You **should** drink milk every day.

shoulder

shoulder

The **shoulder** is the part of the body between the neck and the arm. **shoulders.**

shovel

A **shovel** is a tool used to dig a hole or to scoop something up. I used a snow **shovel** to make a path to the garage. **shovels.**

shovel

show

show   1. Show means to explain or point out something to someone. Kate **showed** me how to skate. **Show** us the toy. **showed, shown, showing.** 2. A **show** is something you watch on TV or at the movies. **shows.**

shown   Max has **shown** us his new kite.

shut   Shut means to close something or to put a cover on something. Ann **shut** the door. **shut, shutting.**

shut

sick

sick   When you are **sick**, you do not feel well. Tim is in bed because he is sick. **sicker, sickest.**

side   1. Side means the edge of something. A triangle has three **sides.** A square has four **sides.** 2. A **side** is also the part of something that is not the top, bottom, front, or back. The **side** of our house is near the fence. **sides.**

side

229

S | s

sidewalk A sidewalk is a place to walk on the side of a street. **sidewalks.**

sidewalk

sign

sign A sign tells you what to do or what not to do. Cars must stop at stop signs. **signs.**

sing When you sing, you make music with your voice. Marco sang a happy song. **sang, sung, singing.**

sink

sink 1. A sink is used to wash things in. Sinks hold water. Ben washed his hands in the sink. **sinks.**
2. Sink also means to go down or under. A rock sinks in water, but wood does not. **sank, sunk, sinking.**

sink

sister Your sister is a girl who has the same mother and father that you have. Maria has a sister. **sisters.**

sister

230

sit When you **sit**, you rest on the lower part of your body with knees bent. We **sat** in our chairs. **sat, sitting.**

sit

size

size The **size** of something is how big or small it is. Dresses come in different **sizes. sizes.**

skate **1.** A **skate** is worn on the foot. An ice **skate** has a sharp blade on it. A roller **skate** has wheels.
2. When you **skate**, you move along on ice skates or roller skates. **skated, skating.**

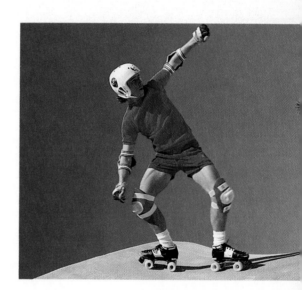

skate

skill A **skill** is something you learn to do by practice. Reading and writing are important **skills. skills.**

skill

skin Skin covers the outside of your body from head to toe. **Skin** helps keep body temperature even.

S | s

skirt

sky

skip Skip means to hop first on one foot and then on the other. When you skip, you can move from place to place. The children **skipped** to their places in line. **skipped, skipping.**

skirt A **skirt** is a kind of clothing that hangs from the waist. **Skirts** can be long or short. They are worn by girls and women. **skirts.**

sky The **sky** is the space far above you when you are outside. Today there was not a cloud in the **sky.**

sled A **sled** is used to slide on snow or ice. We used our **sled** after the first heavy snow this winter. **sleds.**

sled

sleep

sleep I. Sleep means to rest your body. Meg had a dream last night when she was **sleeping. slept, sleeping.** 2. Sleep also means the rest your body needs each night. I try to get eight hours of **sleep** every night.

232

slept   Joe **slept** through the storm.

slide   **1.** A **slide** is something to play on at a playground. You can slip down a **slide** or climb up it. **slides.**
2. Slide also means to move over something easily. Rose **slides** down the hill on her sled. **slid, sliding.**

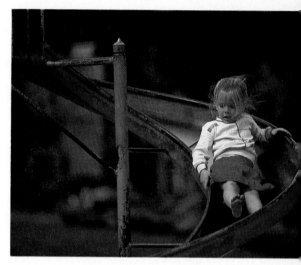

slide

slip   **Slip** means to slide and fall. Mark **slipped** on the ice and broke his arm. **slipped, slipping.**

slip

slow   **1.** Something that is **slow** takes a long time. When something is **slow**, it is not fast. The **slow** runner lost the race. **slower, slowest.**
2. If you **slow** down, you take longer to do things. Al **slowed** down when Bob could not keep up with him. **slowed, slowing.**

slow

small   If something is **small**, it is not large. Chris's sweater has a **small** hole. **smaller, smallest.**

small

S s

smell

smsmell Smell means to use your nose to find out about something. You breathe in when you want to **smell** something. The freshly baked bread **smelled** good. **smelled, smelling.**

smile

smile When you **smile**, the corners of your mouth turn up and you look happy. When Pam made a funny face, I smiled. **smiled, smiling.**

smoke

smoke When something burns, it gives off **smoke**. **Smoke** is made up of the gases that come from the fire. The **smoke** helped the firefighter find the burning apartment.

snack

snack A **snack** is a small amount of food eaten between meals. She had a **snack** after school. **snacks.**

snake A **snake** is a very long and thin animal. **Snakes** have no legs. They move by sliding along the ground. Some **snakes** are small, but some are very long. **snakes.**

snake

sneeze When you **sneeze**, air comes out of your mouth and nose with a loud noise. A person with a cold often sneezes. **sneezed, sneezing.**

sneeze

snow

snow **1.** Snow is frozen drops of water. Soft, white flakes of **snow** come down from the clouds in winter. The **snow** covered the grass in our yard. **2.** Snow also means to come down from the sky in the form of snow. It started to **snow** this morning. **snowed, snowing.**

so The dog seemed hungry, **so** we fed it. I was **so** tired I fell asleep.

soap We use **soap** to wash things and get them clean. We washed our hands with **soap** and water.

soap

soccer Soccer is a game played with a large ball. Players try to kick the ball down the field to win.

soccer

S | s

sock

sock A **sock** is clothing that covers your foot. Beth put on her **socks** and shoes. **socks.**

soft

soft **1.** Something that is **soft** is not hard or stiff. **Soft** things are nice to touch. My teddy bear is very **soft**. **2. Soft** also means not loud. Mother sang to the baby in a **soft** voice. **softer, softest.**

soil

soil Soil is the top layer of the earth. Plants grow in **soil**.

sold Dave **sold** his old bike.

sold

solid Anything that is a **solid** takes up space and has its own shape. It is not a liquid or a gas. Wood and ice are **solids**. **solids.**

some   **Some** of the children jumped rope.
Some animals make good pets.

someone

someone   **Someone** is at the door.

something   There is **something** in my soup.

something

sometimes   **Sometimes** I feel like playing with
friends. **Sometimes** I feel like being
alone.

son

son   A **son** is a boy child. A boy is the
son of his father and mother. The
Smiths have two **sons. sons.**

song   A **song** is music with words. You
can sing a **song. songs.**

soon   **Soon** means in a short time. **Soon** it
will be dark. **sooner, soonest.**

song

Row, Row, Row Your Boat
Traditional Song

Row, row, row your boat

Gent - ly down the stream.

Mer-ri - ly, mer-ri - ly, mer - ri - ly, mer-ri - ly,

Life is but a dream.

S | s

sorry

sorry   When you are **sorry** about something, you feel sad about it. Dan was **sorry** that he missed the baseball game. **sorrier, sorriest.**

sound

sound   A **sound** is something you hear. He heard the **sound** of a bell. **sounds.**

soup

soup   Soup is a kind of liquid food. Mother made **soup** out of water, meat, and vegetables. **soups.**

sour   Something that is **sour** tastes like lemon juice. It does not taste sweet. The cherries were **sour.**

sour

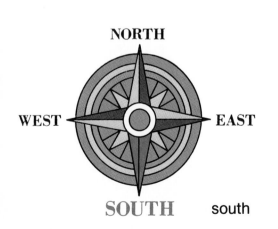
NORTH
WEST   EAST
SOUTH   south

south   South is a direction. If you look at the sun when it comes up, **south** is on your right. **South** is the opposite direction to north.

space   **1.** If there is room for something to fit, there is **space** for it. The puzzle piece was the right shape to fill the space. **spaces.**
2. Space is also the area around the earth. The sun and the stars are in outer **space.**

space

speak   Speak means to say words or to talk. **Speak** louder so I can hear you. **spoke, spoken, speaking.**

speak

special   Something that is **special** is unusual or different. Dad gave me a **special** present for my birthday.

speed

speed   How fast something goes is its **speed.** The jet flew at a faster **speed** than the helicopter. **speeds.**

spell   Spell means to say or write the letters of a word in order. We are learning to **spell** in school. **spelled, spelling.**

D-O-G

spell

S | s

spend

spend
1. Spend means to use money to buy something. How much did you spend at the circus?
2. Spend also means to pass time in some place. Sue will spend a week at the lake. **spent, spending.**

spent
Jack **spent** five dollars at the circus. He **spent** Sunday at home.

spider

spider
A **spider** is a very small animal with eight legs. **Spiders** have no wings and are not insects. Many **spiders** make webs and catch insects in them. **spiders.**

spoke

spoke
Mandy **spoke** to our class today.

spoken
Father has **spoken** to the doctor about Jack's cold.

spoon

spoon We use a **spoon** to eat food. **Spoons** have space at one end to hold the food. We eat cereal with a spoon. **spoons.**

sport A **sport** is a game that needs skill and gives exercise. Basketball and soccer are **sports. sports.**

sport

spread

spread 1. **Spread** means to cover with a thin layer. I **spread** the bread with butter.
2. **Spread** also means to pass on to other people. Sneezes and coughs spread germs. **spread, spreading.**

spring Spring is one of the four seasons. It comes after winter and before summer. The trees get new leaves in the **spring.**

spring

S | s

square
A **square** is a shape. A **square** has four sides, all of the same length. **squares.**

square

squirrel
A **squirrel** is a small animal with a large, furry tail. **Squirrels** live in trees. They like to eat nuts. **squirrels.**

squirrel

stairs
Stairs are a group of steps that go from one floor to another. You can go up and down **stairs.**

stairs

stand
1. **Stand** means to be up on your feet, not sitting down. We **stand** up to read our stories to the class.
2. When something **stands** for something else, it means the same. TV **stands** for television. **stood, standing.**

stand

star **I.** A **star** is something that shines in the sky at night. **Stars** are very far away from the earth.
2. A **star** is also a shape that has five or more points. My teacher drew a **star** on my paper. **stars.**

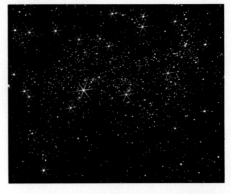

star

start **Start** means to begin to do something. I am going to **start** taking the bus. **started, starting.**

state A **state** is one of the parts of the United States. There are 50 **states.** John's family visited three **states** last summer. **states.**

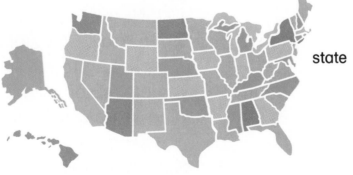

state

stay When you are in the same place for a time, you **stay** there. I **stayed** with my grandmother last week. **stayed, staying.**

stay

stem A **stem** is a part of a plant. Flowers and fruit have **stems.** The trunk of a tree is a **stem. stems.**

stem

243

step

step **1.** Each time you move your foot as you go from place to place, you take a **step.** It is just a few **steps** from here to the kitchen.
2. A **step** is also the place you put your feet when you walk up and down stairs. Billy reached the top **step** without falling. **steps.**

stick¹

stick¹ A **stick** is a long, thin piece of wood. We added **sticks** to the fire. **sticks.**

stick²

stick² **1.** **Stick** means to push something sharp into or through another thing. I **stuck** my fork into the potato.
2. **Stick** also means to make things stay tightly together. John **stuck** the pieces of paper together with glue. **stuck, sticking.**

still Ken is **still** watching TV.

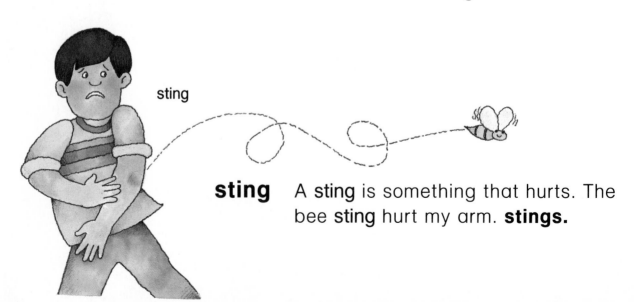

sting

sting A **sting** is something that hurts. The bee **sting** hurt my arm. **stings.**

stomach The food you eat goes into your stomach. Your **stomach** is like a large bag inside your body. **stomachs.**

stomach

stone A **stone** is a small piece of rock. The children threw **stones** into the pond. **stones.**

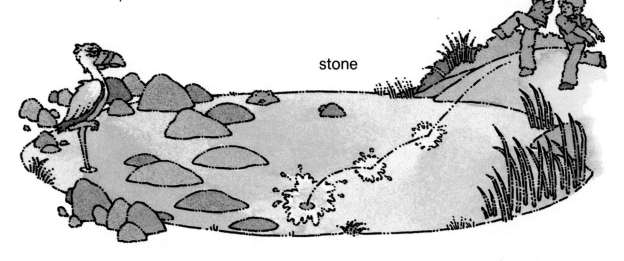

stone

stood We **stood** up to cheer the team.

stop **I.** We **stop** something when we don't do it any more. Jill asked her dad to **stop** smoking.
2. Stop also means to cause something not to move or continue. Drivers **stop** their cars at traffic lights. **stopped, stopping.**

stop

store A **store** is a place to buy things. We drove to the toy **store. stores.**

S | s

storm

story¹

story²

stove

storm   A strong wind with heavy rain or snow is a **storm**. Some **storms** have lightning and thunder. **storms.**

story¹   A **story** tells about people and places and what happens to them. **Stories** can be make-believe or true. Do you know the **story** about the three bears? **stories.**

story²   In a building, a **story** is all the rooms on one floor. Pat's house has two **stories**. **stories.**

stove   A **stove** is used to cook or heat food. There are electric, gas, and wood **stoves**. **stoves.**

straight   Something is **straight** if it does not have a bend or a curve in it. Can you draw a **straight** line? **straighter, straightest.**

straight

stranger   A **stranger** is a person you have not known, seen, or heard of before. Julie was a **stranger** until she met the kids in her class. **strangers.**

straw   A **straw** is used to drink liquids. Straws are made of paper or plastic. **straws.**

straw

stream

stream   A **stream** is running water. A small river is called a **stream**. Max caught a fish in the **stream**. **streams.**

street

street   A **street** is a road in a city or town. I live on this **street**. **streets.**

stretch   When you **stretch** something, you make it as long as it can be. The dog pulled my sweater and stretched it. **stretched, stretching.**

stretch

247

S|s

string

string   A **string** is a long, thin length of twisted threads. It is used to tie things. Ed bought **string** for his new kite. **strings.**

strong   **Strong** means not weak. A **strong** person can move heavy things. Mike was **strong** enough to move the table. **stronger, strongest.**

strong

study

stuck   Tim **stuck** his fork into the potato.

study   We **study** when we try to learn by reading and thinking. Liz **studied** her spelling. **studied, studying.**

subtract

subtract   **Subtract** means to take away. If you **subtract** two from three, you get one. **subtracted, subtracting.**

sudden   Something that happens fast is **sudden.** It is something you did not plan. The train made a **sudden** stop.

sugar Sugar is something sweet to put in food. This cake has **sugar** in it.

sugar

suit A **suit** is a set of clothes that go together. A man's **suit** has a jacket and pants. A woman's **suit** has a jacket and pants or a skirt. **suits.**

suit

summer **Summer** is one of the four seasons. It comes after spring and before fall. **Summer** is the hottest time of the year.

summer

sun The **sun** is a hot ball of gas. It is very far away from the earth. The **sun** gives us heat and light. The earth goes around the **sun.**

sun

sung Many songs were **sung** at camp.

sunk The rock has **sunk** to the bottom of the lake.

sunlight **Sunlight** is the light of the sun. **Sunlight** helps plants to grow.

sunlight

S|s

sunny When the sun shines, it is **sunny**. I like **sunny** days. **sunnier, sunniest.**

sunshine **Sunshine** is the light of the sun. I like to play outside in the **sunshine**.

sunny

sunshine

suppose **I.** If you **suppose** something, you imagine that it is true. **Suppose** you go to the store. What would you buy? I **suppose** I'd buy toys.
2. If you are **supposed** to do something, you should do it. I am **supposed** to go home after school. **supposed, supposing.**

Surprise!

sure When you are **sure** about something, you know you are right. Bob was **sure** that he had fed the dog. **surer, surest.**

surprise **I.** Something that happens that you did not plan is a **surprise**. Tim loved the **surprise** he got for his birthday. **surprises.**
2. We **surprise** someone when we don't tell what is going to happen. We **surprised** Tim by giving him a new bike. **surprised, surprising.**

surprise

swallow When you **swallow** food, you make it go from your mouth to your stomach. Barb **swallowed** the bread slowly. **swallowed, swallowing.**

swam

swam We **swam** at the pool on Saturday.

swan A **swan** is a large, white bird with a long neck. **Swans** live on lakes and rivers. **swans.**

swan

sweater A **sweater** is a kind of clothing that keeps you warm. You can wear a **sweater** over a shirt. **sweaters.**

sweater

sweep **Sweep** means to clean a floor with a broom or a brush. Greg **swept** the floor today. **swept, sweeping.**

sweep

S | s

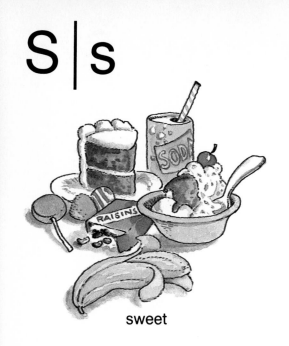
sweet

sweet   Something that tastes like sugar or honey is **sweet**. Most people like sweet food. **sweeter, sweetest.**

swept   Greg **swept** the floor carefully.

swim   **Swim** means to move in the water. People use their arms and legs to swim. **swam, swum, swimming.**

swim

swing   **I.** **Swing** means to move back and forth many times. The girls were **swinging** from the oak tree. **swung, swinging.**
2. A **swing** is something to sit on so you can move back and forth in the air. The **swing** at the playground is too high for me. **swings.**

swing

swum   We had **swum** in the ocean before.

swung   Sue **swung** her arms as she ran.

Tt

table A table has legs and a flat top. You can put things on a table. **tables.**

taco A taco is a kind of food. Tacos are thin corn pancakes filled with chopped meat or chicken and other things. **tacos.**

taco

T | t

tail A **tail** is the part of an animal's body farthest from its head. A fox has a furry **tail. tails.**

tail

take **1.** Take means to get hold of something. **Take** an apple to eat. **2.** Take also means to carry. **Take** the sweater to the game with you. **took, taken, taking.**

taken Jean has **taken** Al to school.

talk

talk Talk means to speak. John is talking to Ruth. **talked, talking.**

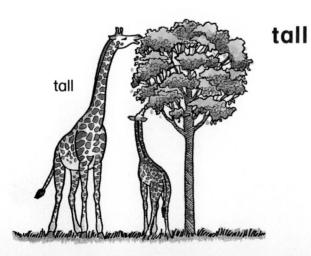

tall

tall When something is **tall**, it reaches a long way from top to bottom. Something **tall** is not short. The **tall** giraffe was as high as the tree. **taller, tallest.**

T | t

tan 1. **Tan** is a color. It is a light, yellowish brown.
2. **Tan** also means to become brown by being in the sun. If you stay on the beach your skin will tan. **tanned, tanning.**

tan

tap Tap means to hit lightly. He **tapped** on the window. **tapped, tapping.**

tape

tape 1. **Tape** is a long piece of paper, plastic, or some other material. Sticky **tape** is used to wrap things.
2. **Tape** also means to make a record on a special plastic tape. He **taped** the movie. **taped, taping.**

taste You **taste** things with your tongue. When you **taste** something, you find out if it is sweet or sour or salty. **tasted, tasting.**

taste

taught Peter **taught** me to play baseball.

taxi A taxi is a car with a driver. The driver is paid to take people from one place to another. **taxis.**

taxi

T | t

teach

teach   Teach means to help someone learn. She **teaches** people how to play the piano. **taught, teaching.**

teacher   A teacher helps people learn. Teachers work in schools. **teachers.**

teacher

team

team   A team is a group of people working or playing together. Sally is on the basketball **team. teams.**

tear   Tear means to pull something into pieces. The baby is **tearing** the newspaper. **tore, torn, tearing.**

tear

teddy bear   A teddy bear is a soft toy bear. Many children like to play with teddy bears. **teddy bears.**

teddy bear

teeth

teeth   Teeth are part of your mouth. Your teeth help you bite and chew food. Each one of your **teeth** is a tooth.

telephone   A **telephone** is used to talk to someone who is in another place. When the **telephone** rang, Kim answered it, and it was Dad. **telephones.**

telephone

telescope

telescope   A **telescope** makes things that are far away seem near. You can look at the stars through a **telescope. telescopes.**

television   When you turn on a **television,** you can see pictures and hear sounds. You can watch shows and movies on television. **televisions.**

television

tell   Tell means to put into words, or to say. Gail likes to **tell** stories. **told, telling.**

temperature   Temperature means how hot or cold something is. The **temperature** outside is warm. **temperatures.**

temperature

T | t

tent

test

thank

tent   A **tent** covers and protects you when you camp outside. It is a large piece of cloth held up by ropes and poles. We slept in a **tent** near the lake. **tents.**

test   A **test** is a way to find out what you know or what you can do. Tests have questions to answer. **tests.**

than   A mountain is bigger **than** a hill. Jane sings better **than** I do.

thank   Thank is a word you use when something pleases you. I **thanked** Cathy for the present. You say "**thank** you" when something has been done for you or given to you. **thanked, thanking.**

that   Who is the owner of **that** bike? I know **that** you are busy.

the   What is **the** name of your dog? **The** cat Betty found is black.

their   **Their** dog is black and mine has spots.

their

them   Ask **them** if they want to play outside. The books were new and I was careful with **them.**

then   Dad used to go running, and he was very thin **then.** We went skating, and **then** we had hot chocolate.

then

there   Sit over **there.** **There** are lots of people in the park.

thermometer   A **thermometer** is used to measure how hot or how cold something is. We looked at the **thermometer** to see how hot it was. Mom took my temperature with a **thermometer.** **thermometers.**

thermometer

T | t

these   Manuel read **these** books. **These** are his books and those are mine.

they   Luis and Maria came home late because **they** stopped to play.

thick

thick   When something is **thick**, it is not thin. A **thick** object is wide from one side to the other. The blue book is thick. **thicker, thickest.**

thin   **1.** When something is **thin**, it is not wide from one side to the other. Something **thin** is not thick. A sheet of paper is **thin**.
2. **Thin** also means having little fat on the body. John is very **thin**. **thinner, thinnest.**

thin

thing

thing   Don't leave that **thing** on the floor. Please put your **things** away. That is not a nice **thing** to do. **things.**

think **1.** When you **think**, you use your mind. I had to **think** before answering the question.
2. Think also means to believe. Do you **think** it will rain? We **think** it might snow. **thought, thinking.**

third

third **Third** means next after the second. The **third** letter of the alphabet is C.

thirsty

thirsty **Thirsty** means needing something to drink. The popcorn made me thirsty. **thirstier, thirstiest.**

this **This** is my jacket and that is my brother's jacket. **This** year I am six.

those May bought **those** books. **Those** are her books and these are mine.

thought

thought Jim **thought** about which record to buy. We **thought** it was raining.

T | t

thread   Thread is very thin string. You sew clothes with **thread**. **threads.**

thread

threw   Kate **threw** the ball over the fence.

through   The bird flew **through** the house. Are you **through** with your dinner?

through

throw   Throw means to send something through the air. **Throw** the ball to me. **threw, thrown, throwing.**

throw

thrown   He has **thrown** the ball already.

thumb

thumb   The **thumb** is the short, thick finger on each of your hands. **thumbs.**

thunder

thunder   Thunder is the loud noise that often follows lightning. My cat is afraid of thunder.

tie Tie means to hold something together by putting string or rope around it. She **tied** the package with white string. **tied, tying.**

tie

tiger

tiger A **tiger** is a large animal that looks like a cat. **Tigers** have yellow fur with black stripes. **tigers.**

time Time is always going by. Seconds, minutes, hours, days, months, and years are ways we measure **time**. Clocks tell us what **time** it is.

time

tiny

tiny Tiny means very small. Tiny bugs are hard to see. **tinier, tiniest.**

tip¹ Tip means the end part. She cut the **tip** of her finger. **tips.**

tip¹

tip² Tip means to turn over. The boat tipped over. **tipped, tipping.**

T | t

tire A tire fits around a wheel. **Tires** are filled with air. A car has four **tires. tires.**

tire

tired **Tired** means feeling worn out and ready to rest. Running made me tired.

tired

title

title **1.** A **title** is the name of a book, poem, picture, or song. The **title** of this fairy tale is ''Cinderella.''
2. A **title** is also a name telling what a person is or does. ''Mayor'' and ''prince'' are **titles. titles.**

to Are you going **to** the beach? What do you want **to** take?

today **Today** means this day. **Today** I am going to the zoo.

toe

toe A **toe** is a part of the foot. Each foot has five **toes. toes.**

together Let's all go **together** to the lake.

together

told My mother **told** me to be quiet.

told

tomato A **tomato** is a round, red fruit. Tomatoes are juicy. They grow on vines. **tomatoes.**

tomato

tomorrow Tomorrow is the day after today. We'll go shopping **tomorrow.**

tongue Your **tongue** is part of your mouth. It moves and bends to help you say words. Your **tongue** also helps you taste food. **tongues.**

tongue

tonight Tonight means this night. I am going to the movies **tonight.**

T | t

took

tooth

tool

too   She felt **too** sad to go to the party. I was tired, and I was hungry **too**.

took   My brother **took** us to school today.

tool   A **tool** is something that helps you do work. A saw is a **tool**. **tools.**

tooth   A **tooth** is one of the hard, white parts in your mouth. You bite and chew food with your **teeth**. **teeth.**

toothbrush

toothbrush   A toothbrush is a brush used to clean your teeth. **toothbrushes.**

top¹

top¹   Top means the highest part. We saw the **top** of the mountain. **tops.**

top²   A **top** is a toy that spins. The **top** went round and round. **tops.**

top²

tore

tore   I **tore** my jeans climbing a tree.

torn   The picture was **torn** in half.

torn

touch   **Touch** means to feel something with your hand. Chris **touched** the cat's soft fur. **touched, touching.**

touch

toward   We drove **toward** home.

towel   A **towel** is a piece of cloth used to dry someone or something. Dry the dishes with a **towel**. **towels.**

towel

town   A **town** is a large group of houses and other buildings. A **town** is smaller than a city. **towns.**

toy   A **toy** is something to play with. Teddy bears and tops are **toys**. **toys.**

toy

T | t

trace   Trace means to copy by following letters or lines with a pen or pencil. He put paper over the map and traced it. **traced, tracing.**

trace

track   A track is what the wheels of a train run on. The train **tracks** go through the center of town. **tracks.**

track

traffic   Traffic is cars, trucks, and buses moving along at the same time. There is a lot of **traffic** on this road.

traffic

train   A **train** is used to carry people and goods from one place to another. A **train** runs on a track and has many cars hooked together. An engine at the front makes the **train** go. **trains.**

train

travel   Travel means to go from one place to another. They hope to **travel** next summer. **traveled, traveling.**

tree A **tree** is a big plant. It has a trunk, branches, and leaves. Some **trees** have fruit that we eat. **trees.**

tree

triangle A **triangle** is a shape. A **triangle** has three sides. **triangles.**

triangle

trick A **trick** is something done to make people laugh or to fool them. A **trick** is also something you can teach an animal to do. Fran's dog can roll over and do other **tricks. tricks.**

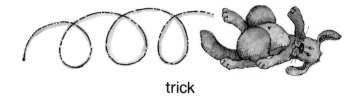

trick

trip **1.** When you go on a **trip**, you travel from one place to another. Let's take a **trip** to the ocean. **trips.**
2. Trip also means to fall. I **tripped** on the rope. **tripped, tripping.**

truck A **truck** is a machine that can carry heavy loads. It has a motor and wheels. **Trucks** are bigger than cars. **trucks.**

truck

T | t

true True means right or correct. It is **true** that 4 and 6 are 10. A **true** story is not made up. **truer, truest.**

trunk

trunk **1.** A **trunk** is a part of a tree. The branches and roots grow from the **trunk**. Trees have bark on their trunks.
2. A **trunk** is also a part of an elephant that looks like a very long nose. Elephants carry food to their mouths with their **trunks**. **trunks.**

try

try Try means to set out to do something if you can. **Try** to hit the ball. **tried, trying.**

tube

tube A tube is used to hold things such as toothpaste or paint. **Tubes** are made of plastic or thin metal. They have a cap on one end. **tubes.**

tulip

tulip A tulip is a flower shaped like a cup. **Tulips** come in many colors. They bloom in the spring. **tulips.**

turkey   A **turkey** is a large bird with brown or white feathers. **Turkeys** have long necks. **turkeys.**

turkey

turn   **1.** Turn means to move around a center as a wheel does. The record kept turning. **turned, turning.**
2. Turn also means a chance to do something. It is her **turn** to read. **turns.**

turn

turtle

turtle   A **turtle** is an animal with a soft body and a hard shell. **Turtles** live both in water and on land. **Turtles** can be small or large. **turtles.**

TV   TV means television. I watched TV after dinner. **TVs.**

twin   A **twin** is one of two children born to the same parents at the same time. Joe and Al are **twins. twins.**

twin

271

Uu

umbrella An **umbrella** is something you hold over your head to keep yourself dry when it rains. Mike's **umbrella** is made of cloth, but Ann's is made of plastic. **umbrellas.**

umbrella

U | u

uncle   Your **uncle** is your father's brother or your mother's brother. Your aunt's husband is also your **uncle**. **uncles.**

under   The ball rolled **under** the chair. Joe can buy the skates he wants for **under** ten dollars.

under

underline   When we draw a line under something, we **underline** it. The teacher asked us to **underline** the correct answer. **underlined, underlining.**

$$2 + 2 = ? \qquad 3 \ 5 \ \underline{4} \ 7$$

underline

understand   You **understand** something when you know what it means. Bob listened carefully so he could **understand** the directions. **understood, understanding.**

understood   Sue **understood** the rules of the game after Ann explained them.

understood

U | u

unhappy

Unhappy means sad. When Jim's best friend moved away, he felt unhappy. **unhappier, unhappiest.**

unhappy

unicorn

unicorn

A unicorn is a make-believe animal. A unicorn looks like a horse with a long horn in the front of its head. **unicorns.**

unit

A unit is a special part of something. The first unit of our science book is about the human body. **units.**

until

Will couldn't wait until his birthday. He did not open his presents until his dad came home.

until

unusual

unusual

Something that does not happen often is unusual. It is unusual to see a horse wearing a hat.

up

The price of candy went up. The cat ran up the tree. We got up at seven o'clock. Your time is up now.

up

upon   Ann fell asleep **upon** her mother's lap. Once **upon** a time there was a dragon who was scared.

upon

us   Many of **us** played outside after lunch. The teacher called **us** when it was time to come inside.

use   Vera and I can **use** our tools to build a doghouse. Brian will **use** all the wood we have. **used, using.**

use

useful   When something is **useful**, it helps us. The hammer and saw were **useful** when we built the doghouse.

useful

usual   When something happens often, it is **usual**. Snow is **usual** here in the winter.

Vv

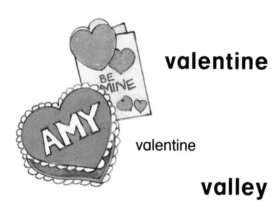

valentine

valentine

A valentine is a card or a small present that you send or receive on Valentine's Day. Amy received two **valentines**. **valentines.**

valley

valley

A valley is the low area between mountains or hills. Rivers often run through **valleys**. **valleys.**

van   A **van** is a covered truck used to carry people or things. We used our **van** to go on a camping trip. **vans.**

van

vase

vase   A **vase** is used to hold flowers. Jan filled the **vase** with tulips. **vases.**

vegetable   A **vegetable** is a plant used for food. Peas, corn, lettuce, and beans are **vegetables. vegetables.**

vegetable

very   Jerry was **very** hungry. He had a **very** large dinner.

village   A **village** is a small town. There are few houses in a **village. villages.**

village

V | v

vine   A **vine** is a plant that grows along the ground. Some **vines** climb up walls and fences. Pumpkins and grapes grow on **vines. vines.**

vine

violin

violin   A **violin** is used to make music. A **violin** is made of wood and has four strings. You push and pull a stick called a bow across the strings to make sounds. **violins.**

visit

visit   When you go to see places or people, you **visit** them. Ann wanted to **visit** her aunt. **visited, visiting.**

voice

voice   Your **voice** is the sound you make with your mouth. You use your **voice** to talk and sing. **voices.**

Ww

wagon A **wagon** can carry people or things. **Wagons** have four wheels. Sam's dog rode in the **wagon. wagons.**

wagon

W w

wait
Wait means to stay where you are. People **wait** for something to happen or for someone to come. We **waited** a long time for May and Billy to come. **waited, waiting.**

wait

wake
When you **wake**, you stop sleeping. What time did you **wake** up? **woke, woken, waking.**

wake

walk
Walk means to move by putting one foot in front of the other. I **walked** to school. **walked, walking.**

walk

wall
A **wall** is the side of a building or room. Ruth will paint the **walls** of her room blue. **walls.**

want
When you **want** something, you would like to have it or to do it. I want a kitten. **wanted, wanting.**

want

280

warm   Warm means more hot than cold. It's a **warm** day. I felt **warm** by the fire. **warmer, warmest.**

warm

was   Her dog **was** gone. She **was** sad.

wash   Wash means to clean with soap and water. Joan **washed** her hands before lunch. **washed, washing.**

wash

watch

watch   **1.** Watch means to look at something or someone. Watch how I do this. **watched, watching.**
2. Watch also means a small clock you wear on your wrist. **watches.**

water   Water is the liquid that fills the ocean, rivers, lakes, and ponds. Water falls from the sky as rain. People and animals need **water** to live.

water

W | w

wave

wave When the water in an ocean or lake rises and moves forward, it forms a wave. I saw the big **waves**. **waves.**

way **I.** How something is done is the **way** it is done. This is the **way** I draw a tree.
2. Way also means the direction you follow to get to a place. Is this the **way** to Ben's house? **ways.**

we

we I met Jane, and **we** went skating.

wear

wear When you **wear** something, you have it on your body. **Wear** your brown jacket today. **wore, worn, wearing.**

weather How it is outside is the **weather**. The wind, the air temperature, and how wet or dry it is tell us what the **weather** is like. The **weather** today is sunny and warm.

weather

web

web   A **web** is made by a spider to catch insects for food. **Webs** look like nets made of very fine thread. **webs.**

week   A **week** is a way to measure time. It has seven days. The days of the **week** are Sunday, Monday, Tuesday, Wednesday, Thursday, Friday, and Saturday. A year has 52 weeks. **weeks.**

week

weigh   **Weigh** means to find out how heavy a person or thing is. I **weighed** the apples. **weighed, weighing.**

weigh

well   **1.** **Well** means in a fine way. Kay does her work **well**. **better, best.** **2.** **Well** also means in good health. Ed felt sick, but now he feels **well**.

well

went   Sue **went** to the store.

were   They **were** cleaning the house. We **were** sorry it rained.

283

W | w

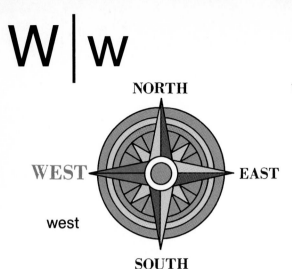

NORTH

WEST — EAST

west

SOUTH

west   West is a direction. The sun sets in the **west**. **West** is the opposite direction to east.

wet   When something is **wet**, it is full of water. Lee's hair is **wet**, but Kate's is dry. **wetter, wettest.**

wet

whale   A **whale** is a very large animal that lives in the sea. **Whales** are not fish. **whales.**

whale

wheel

what   **What** is his name? Liz doesn't know **what** to do.

wheel   A **wheel** is round. It turns around its center. **Wheels** help things move and work. Cars have four **wheels**. Bicycles have two **wheels**. **wheels.**

when   **When** are you leaving?

W | w

where   Where did you put your gloves? I know **where** they are.

which   Which book do you want to read? I don't know **which** way to go.

which

whistle   When you **whistle**, you make a clear, high sound by blowing air through your teeth or lips. Jim **whistled** for his dog. **whistled, whistling.**

whistle

white   White is a color. Snow is **white.**

white

who   Who is going to the ball game? Tell me **who** was at the party.

whole

whole   Whole means not having any parts missing. The **whole** class is here. There is only one **whole** apple left.

W | w

wide

win

why Why are you sad? Tell Mom the reason **why** you are sad.

wide When something is **wide**, it is big from side to side. The road to town is **wide**. The ocean is very **wide**. **wider, widest.**

wig A **wig** is a covering of hair for the head. She puts on a red **wig** when she dresses as a clown. **wigs.**

wig

wild

wild Wild means not raised or grown by people. **Wild** animals live in the forest. **Wild** flowers grow in the woods. **wilder, wildest.**

will I will be able to go to the party. Sue **will** ask her mom to drive me.

win You **win** when you are better than others at doing something. You **win** when you are the best. Our team **won** the game. **won, winning.**

wind Wind is moving air. The **wind** blew leaves off the trees. **winds.**

wind

window A **window** is an open space in a wall. **Windows** are made of glass and can be opened. A **window** lets light and fresh air into a building. **windows.**

window

windy When it is **windy**, there is a lot of wind. It is **windy** at the ocean. **windier, windiest.**

wing A **wing** is a part of a bird, insect, or bat. **Wings** move and are used in flying. **wings.**

wing

winter

winter Winter is one of the four seasons. It comes after fall and before spring. Winter is the coldest time of the year.

W | w

wish   Wish means to want something. He wished for a bike. **wished, wishing.**

wish

witch

witch   A witch is a make-believe person. In stories, witches sometimes fly on brooms. **witches.**

with   Do you want to go with us? I cut the meat with a knife.

without

without   Don't go out without a coat.

woke

woke   She woke up early this morning. She was noisy and woke up the whole family.

woken   She has woken up early again.

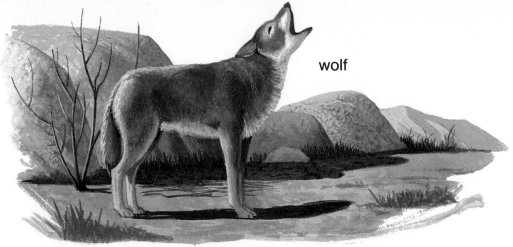

wolf

wolf   A **wolf** is an animal that looks like a large dog. **Wolves** live together in large groups. **wolves.**

wolves   We heard the cries of the **wolves**.

woman   A girl grows up to be a **woman**. Girls grow up to be **women**. **women.**

woman

women   These girls will become **women**.

won   Who **won** the football game?

wood   The trunk and branches of a tree are made of **wood**. **Wood** is used to build houses and make paper.

wood

woods

woods   **Woods** means a lot of trees and bushes growing together. There are many kinds of trees in the **woods**.

W | w

word A **word** is a sound or group of sounds that means something. People speak and write **words**. **words.**

wore Jim **wore** new shoes to the party.

work
1. **Work** is a job you do. Driving a truck is hard **work**.
2. **Work** means to do a job. Lisa **worked** hard shoveling snow. **worked, working.**

work

worker

worker A **worker** is someone who works. Lisa is a good **worker**. **workers.**

world

world The **world** is the earth and everything on it.

worm

worm A **worm** is a small, thin animal with a soft body. **Worms** have no legs and move by creeping. **worms.**

worn He has **worn** that jacket often.

worn

worse Stan's cold is **worse** today.

worse   worst

worst It is the **worst** cold he ever had.

would **Would** you like some candy? She said she **would** come to the party.

wrist The **wrist** is the part of the body between the hand and the arm. **wrists.**

wrist

write **Write** means to make letters and words with a pen or pencil. Can you **write** your name? **wrote, written, writing.**

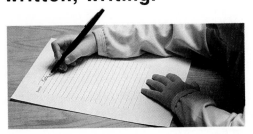

write

written She has **written** a letter to her aunt.

wrong **Wrong** means not right or not true. It was **wrong** of him to take my book. She gave the **wrong** answer.

wrong

wrote Lynn **wrote** a poem.

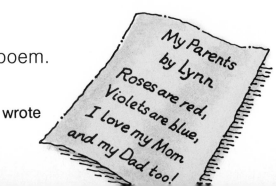

wrote

My Parents
by Lynn
Roses are red,
Violets are blue,
I love my Mom
and my Dad too!

X x

X ray

X ray

An **X ray** is a picture that shows what is inside something. **X rays** can tell you if you have broken bones. They can tell you if you have any cavities in your teeth. My doctor took an **X ray** of my arm. **X rays.**

xylophone

A xylophone is used to make music. You hit the **xylophone** with wooden hammers to make different sounds. **xylophones.**

xylophone

Y y

yak A **yak** is a large animal with long hair. **Yaks** live in cold places. **yaks.**

yak

Y | y

yard

yard A **yard** is a piece of ground next to a house or a school. A **yard** may have a fence around it. Mother let us play outside, but we could not leave the **yard. yards.**

yarn

yarn Yarn is a kind of thread. It is used for knitting. Rosa lost her ball of **yarn** and her kitten found it.

yawn

yawn When you **yawn,** you open your mouth wide to get more air. People **yawn** when they are tired and need some sleep. **yawned, yawning.**

year

year A **year** is a way to measure time. A **year** has twelve months. The new **year** starts on January 1. Bobby is ten **years** old. **years.**

yell   **I.** Yell means to cry out with a strong, loud sound. Nick **yelled** for help when he saw the fire. **yelled, yelling.**
2. Yell also means a strong, loud cry. Nick's **yell** made his mother call the firefighters. **yells.**

yell

yellow   Yellow is a color. Lemons and butter are **yellow.**

yellow

yes   When Sally says **yes** to something, she wants to do it. When Kevin asked her to come over, she said, "**Yes.**"

yes

yesterday   Yesterday is the day before today. We visited Grandpa **yesterday.**

you   You have two sisters and I have one. **You** have more sisters than I do.

Y | y

young

yoyo

young   Young means to be in the early part of life. **Young** is the opposite of old. A puppy is a **young** dog. A baby is a **young** child. **younger, youngest.**

your   **Your** toys belong to you. If you tell me **your** name, I will tell you mine.

yours   This toy is mine, and that toy is **yours**. This pencil is his, and that one is **yours**.

yours

yourself   Can you teach **yourself** the words to a song? Can you sing it all by **yourself?**

yoyo   A **yoyo** is a toy made of two round pieces joined together. A string is tied to a **yoyo**. The **yoyo** goes up and down along the string. **yoyos.**

Zz

zebra A **zebra** is an animal that looks like a horse. **Zebras** have black and white stripes. **zebras.**

zebra

Z z

zero

zero   **I.** Zero is the number 0. If you put a **zero** after the number I, you get the number 10. **zeros.**
2. Zero also means none at all. The score was nine to **zero.**

zip[1]   Zip means to move or act quickly. The cars **zipped** out of the parking area. **zipped, zipping.**

zip[2]   Zip means to close something with a zipper. Al **zipped** up his jacket before he went outside. **zipped, zipping.**

zipper

zipper   A **zipper** is used to hold things together. Sweaters, jackets, pants, and skirts can have **zippers.** Does your jacket have buttons or a zipper? **zippers.**

zoo   A **zoo** is a place where all kinds of animals are kept. People visit the **zoo** to see the animals. The **zoo** in our city asks us not to feed the animals. **zoos.**

zoo

Shapes

Find Out the Facts!

Can you find these shapes?

○ circle
□ square
▭ rectangle
△ triangle
☆ star
⬡ octagon

Numbers, Measurement

1	one
2	two
3	three
4	four
5	five
6	six
7	seven
8	eight
9	nine
10	ten
11	eleven
12	twelve
13	thirteen
14	fourteen
15	fifteen
16	sixteen
17	seventeen
18	eighteen
19	nineteen
20	twenty

centimeters— 0 1 2 3 4 5 6 7 8 9 10

inches— 0 1 2 3 4

12 inches equal 1 foot

I slice of bread weighs about
I ounce

16 ounces equal
I pound

I kilogram is a little more than 2 pounds

I cup

I pint
2 cups

I quart
2 pints
4 cups

I gallon
4 quarts
8 pints
16 cups

I liter
is a little
more than
I quart

Time

Parts of the Body

hair

ear

eye

nose

mouth

chin

neck

shoulder

elbow

chest

arm

hand

finger

thumb

wrist

stomach

heel

foot

leg

knee

ankle

toe

Healthy Snacks

Choose healthy foods when you want to eat a snack.
Stay away from foods that have a lot of salt.
Stay away from foods that have a lot of sugar.

Finding Places

State	U.S. Post Office Abbreviation	State Capital
◼ Alabama	AL	Montgomery
◼ Alaska	AK	Juneau
◻ Arizona	AZ	Phoenix
◻ Arkansas	AR	Little Rock
◼ California	CA	Sacramento
◼ Colorado	CO	Denver
◻ Connecticut	CT	Hartford
◼ Delaware	DE	Dover
◼ Florida	FL	Tallahassee
◼ Georgia	GA	Atlanta
◼ Hawaii	HI	Honolulu
◼ Idaho	ID	Boise
◼ Illinois	IL	Springfield
◼ Indiana	IN	Indianapolis
◼ Iowa	IA	Des Moines
◼ Kansas	KS	Topeka
◻ Kentucky	KY	Frankfort
◼ Louisiana	LA	Baton Rouge
◼ Maine	ME	Augusta
◼ Maryland	MD	Annapolis
◼ Massachusetts	MA	Boston
◻ Michigan	MI	Lansing
◼ Minnesota	MN	St. Paul
◼ Mississippi	MS	Jackson
◻ Missouri	MO	Jefferson City

State	U.S. Post Office Abbreviation	State Capital
◼ Montana	MT	Helena
◻ Nebraska	NE	Lincoln
◼ Nevada	NV	Carson City
◼ New Hampshire	NH	Concord
◼ New Jersey	NJ	Trenton
◼ New Mexico	NM	Santa Fe
◼ New York	NY	Albany
◼ North Carolina	NC	Raleigh
◼ North Dakota	ND	Bismarck
◻ Ohio	OH	Columbus
◼ Oklahoma	OK	Oklahoma City
◻ Oregon	OR	Salem
◼ Pennsylvania	PA	Harrisburg
◼ Rhode Island	RI	Providence
◼ South Carolina	SC	Columbia
◼ South Dakota	SD	Pierre
◼ Tennessee	TN	Nashville
◼ Texas	TX	Austin
◼ Utah	UT	Salt Lake City
◼ Vermont	VT	Montpelier
◼ Virginia	VA	Richmond
◼ Washington	WA	Olympia
◼ West Virginia	WV	Charleston
◻ Wisconsin	WI	Madison
◼ Wyoming	WY	Cheyenne

Countries of the World

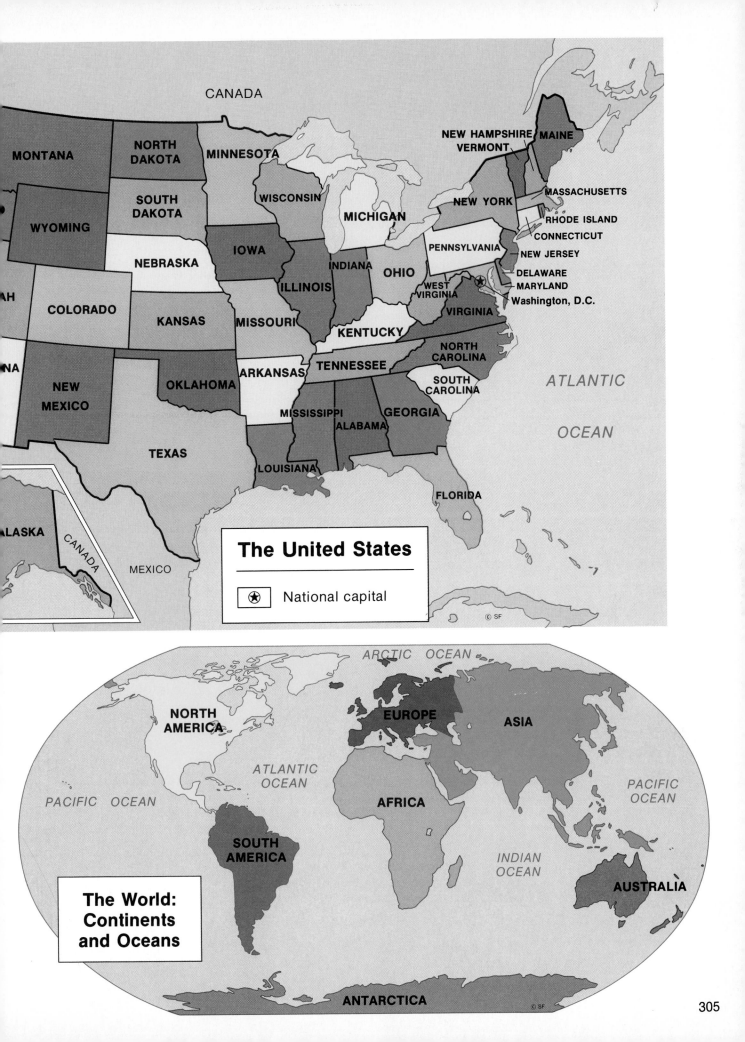

The United States

⊛ National capital

CANADA

MONTANA
NORTH DAKOTA
MINNESOTA
NEW HAMPSHIRE
MAINE
VERMONT
WYOMING
SOUTH DAKOTA
WISCONSIN
MICHIGAN
NEW YORK
MASSACHUSETTS
RHODE ISLAND
CONNECTICUT
NEBRASKA
IOWA
INDIANA
OHIO
PENNSYLVANIA
NEW JERSEY
UTAH
ILLINOIS
DELAWARE
MARYLAND
COLORADO
KANSAS
MISSOURI
WEST VIRGINIA
Washington, D.C.
VIRGINIA
KENTUCKY
ARIZONA
NEW MEXICO
OKLAHOMA
ARKANSAS
TENNESSEE
NORTH CAROLINA
SOUTH CAROLINA
MISSISSIPPI
GEORGIA
ALABAMA
TEXAS
LOUISIANA
FLORIDA

ATLANTIC OCEAN

ALASKA
CANADA
MEXICO

© SF

The World: Continents and Oceans

ARCTIC OCEAN

NORTH AMERICA
EUROPE
ASIA
ATLANTIC OCEAN
PACIFIC OCEAN
AFRICA
PACIFIC OCEAN
SOUTH AMERICA
INDIAN OCEAN
AUSTRALIA
ANTARCTICA

© SF

305

Calendar

Days of the Week

Sunday
Monday
Tuesday
Wednesday
Thursday
Friday
Saturday

Months of the Year

January
February
March
April
May
June
July
August
September
October
November
December

The name of the month is written here.

Month

Sunday	Monday	Tuesday	Wednesday	Thursday	Friday	Saturday
	1	2	3	4	5	6
7	8	9	10	11	12	13
14	15	16	17	18	19	20
21	22	23	24	25	26	27
28	29	30 Holiday				

The days of the week are listed here.

Each day of the week has a number. The numbers are in order.

Holidays happen on different days and in different months throughout the year. On some holidays, people do not go to work.

Holidays

January 1

New Year's Day is the first day of the new year.

January

Martin Luther King Day is on the third Monday in January.

February 14

On Valentine's Day, we send cards to people we love.

February

Presidents' Day is the third Monday in February. It honors George Washington and Abraham Lincoln.

March or April

At Easter, Christians mark the return to life of Jesus. It is a Sunday in March or April.

March or April

Passover is a Jewish holiday that comes in the spring. It lasts eight days. It marks the escape of the Jews from slavery.

May

Memorial Day honors Americans who died in war. It is the last Monday in May.

July 4

On Independence Day, Americans started a new country.

September

Labor Day honors working people. It is the first Monday in September.

October 12

Columbus Day honors Christopher Columbus. On this day in 1492 he first arrived in America.

October 31

On Halloween, people carve pumpkins and trick or treat.

November

Thanksgiving is the fourth Thursday in November. On this day we give thanks for what we have received.

December

On Hanukkah, the festival of lights, Jewish children give gifts and light candles.

December 25

Christians mark the birth of Jesus at Christmas.

Opposites

Can you pair the opposites in this picture?

above

high

below

thick

thin

clean

cold

dirty

hot

on

off

sad

closed

open

asleep

more

low

empty

awake

less

full

high/low   thick/thin   more/less
above/below   clean/dirty   empty/full
on/off   asleep/awake   closed/open
hot/cold

over

under

left   right

happy

tall

outside   inside

short

small   large

big   little   top

in

soft

bottom

out

hard

wet

dry

over/under   in/out   big/little
happy/sad   left/right   top/bottom
small/large   tall/short   wet/dry
hard/soft   outside/inside

Colors

red
+ yellow
= orange

yellow
+ blue
= green

blue
+ red
= purple

red

yellow

blue

black

red

brown

black
+ white
= gray

red
+ white
= pink

brown
+ white
= tan

Credits

Cover Illustration by Lee Lee Brazeal

Other illustrations by

Michael Adams, Ed Aitchinson, Liz Allen, Robert Alley, Randal Birkey, Tom Bobroski, Deborah Borgo, Robin Brickman, Nan Brooks, Helen Davie, Andrea Eberbach, Keith Freeman, Fred Harsh, Jeanne Heitkamp, Jean Helmer, Celeste Henriquez, Pat G. Hinton, Alan Jansen, G. Brian Karas, Diana Magnuson, Cynthia Maniates, Dick Martin, Kathleen Dunn McCarthy, Jane McReary, Robert Masheris, Larry Mikec, Stephen Moore, Nancy Munger, Cathy Pavia, Ondre Pettingill, Joe Rogers, Eileen Rosen, Ed Sauk, Meyer Seltzer, Georgia Shola, Joel Snyder, Josef Sumichrast, Ed Taber, Justin Wager, Jack Wallen, Jan Wills, Lane Yerkes.

All photographs not credited are the property of Scott, Foresman.

animal: The Brooklyn Museum, Dick S. Ramsay Fund
artist: Printed by permission of the Estate of Norman Rockwell, Copyright © 1960 Estate of Norman Rockwell
astronaut: NASA
ate: Jay Johnson America's Folk Heritage Gallery, New York City
autumn: L. West/FPG
bell: FPG
boat: Smithsonian Institution
bounce: David R. Frazier/Frazier Photolibrary
bridge: The Granger Collection, New York
bright: Bill Ross/Aperture PhotoBank
cactus John Gerlach/Earth Scenes
capital: Arthur Grace/Stock, Boston
castle: D. & J. Heaton/Stock, Boston
cave: John L. Pontier/Earth Scenes
church: Bob Daemmrich/Stock, Boston
city: J. Blank/FPG
clay: Alan Oddie/PhotoEdit
cloud: Joseph Nettis/Stock, Boston
clown: Willinger/FPG
earth: NASA
evening: B. Christensen/Stock, Boston
factory: David R. Frazier/Frazier Photolibrary
fast: Focus on Sports
father: Dennis Hallinan/FPG
flower: Scala/Art Resource, NY
fly²: Dan McCoy/Rainbow
grape: Charlton Photos
grow: (all) Brent Jones

haystack: The Granger Collection, New York
horse: Tate/Art Resource, NY
ice: The Harry T. Peters Collection, Museum of the City of New York
jet: Bill Gillette/Stock, Boston
kiss: Richard Dunoff/The Stock Market
kitchen: Paul von Stroheim/West Light
lake: Richard Harrington/FPG
land: J. Zimmerman/FPG
lightning: J. W. Myers/Stock, Boston
man: David W. Hamilton/The Image Bank
mom: Lawrence Migdale/Stock, Boston
moon: Don Landwehrle/The Image Bank
motor: Charles Allen/The Image Bank
mountain: Jose Carrillo/Stock, Boston
net: David Stoecklein/The Stock Market
nurse: Jon Feingersh/Stock, Boston
ocean: The Granger Collection, New York
office: Jeffrey Sylvester/FPG
old: Elizabeth Crews/Stock, Boston
parade: Gabe Palmer/The Stock Market
piano: Gabe Palmer/The Stock Market
pilot: Morton Beebe/The Image Bank
queen: Private Collection
rainbow: Manuel S. Morales/The Image Bank
real: Stephen Brown/The Stock Market
robot: Karen Kent/The Stock Market
sail: Sharon Green/The Stock Market
school: Michael Mauney:TSW-CLICK/Chicago
scientist: Chris Jones/The Stock Market
sister: David Stoecklein/The Stock Market
skate: Carroll Seghers/The Stock Market

sky: Gary Irving:TSW-CLICK/Chicago
slide: Tibor Bognar/The Stock Market
soccer: Charles Krebs/The Stock Market
spring: The Granger Collection, New York
star: David Jeffrey/The Image Bank
storm: Leverett Bradley/FPG
sun: M. Keller/FPG
swam: Ellis Herwig/The Picture Cube
swan: Adolf Schmidecker/FPG
team: Collection of Catherine Bridgman
traffic: Pete Saloutos:TSW-CLICK/Chicago
truck: Chris Jones/The Stock Market
twin: Whitney Lane/The Image Bank
unicorn: The Metropolitan Museum of Art, Gift of John D. Rockefeller, Jr., The Cloisters Collection, 1937
valley: Craig Aurness/West Light
van: John Scheiber/The Stock Market
village: Stephen R. Brown/The Stock Market
violin: Don Perdue/Gamma-Liaison
water: (l) TSW-CLICK/Chicago
(c l) Anne Heimann/The Stock Market
(c r) William A. Logan/The Image Bank
(r) Fridmar Damm/Leo de Wys Inc.
wave: The Granger Collection, New York
wide: TSW-CLICK/Chicago
win: Paul Barton/The Stock Market
winter: The Granger Collection, New York
woods: Cathlyn Melloan:TSW-CLICK/Chicago
world: NASA

311

The D'Nealian® Alphabet

a b c d e f
g h i j k l
m n o p q r
s t u v w x y z
A B C D E F
G H I J K L
M N O P Q R
S T U V W
X Y Z , ' . ?
1 2 3 4 5
6 7 8 9 10